MELVYN BRAGG

Melvyn Bragg was born in Wigton, Cumbria in 1939. His first novel, FOR WANT OF A NAIL, was published in 1965. Since then he has written twelve further novels, several works of non-fiction which include his bestselling biography of Richard Burton, RICH, and LAND OF THE LAKES, as well as a story for children entitled A CHRISTMAS CHILD. Many of his novels, including THE MAID OF BUTTERMERE, are set in his native region, as is A TIME TO DANCE. He has also written the screenplay for the BBC television dramatisation of this, his latest novel.

Controller of Arts at London Weekend Television where he has edited and presented *The South Bank Show* since its inception in 1978, he is also Chairman of Border Television and President of the National Campaign for the Arts. Married to the television director Cate Haste and with three children, he lives in London and Cumbria.

sceptre

MELVYN BRAGG

A Time to Dance

sceptre

First published in Great Britain in
1990 by Hodder and Stoughton
Ltd

Sceptre edition 1991
This format 1992

Sceptre is an imprint of Hodder
and Stoughton Paperbacks, a division of Hodder and Stoughton Ltd

Printed and bound in Great Britain
for Hodder and Stoughton Paper-
backs, a division of Hodder and
Stoughton Ltd, Mill Road, Dunton
Green, Sevenoaks, Kent TN13
2YA. (Editorial Office: 47 Bedford
Square, London WC1B 3DP) by
Clays Ltd, St Ives plc. Photoset by
Rowland Phototypesetting Ltd,
Bury St Edmunds, Suffolk.

British Library C.I.P.

Bragg, Melvyn, *1939–*
A time to dance.
I. Title
823'.914[F]

ISBN 0-340-56848-8

To Nick Elliott

To everything there is a season, and a time to every purpose under heaven:
A time to be born, and a time to die; a time to plant, and a time to pluck up that which is planted;
A time to kill, and a time to heal; a time to break down, and a time to build up;
A time to weep, and a time to laugh; a time to mourn, and a time to dance . . .

Ecclesiastes 3:i–iv

'All this is madness,' cries a sober sage:
But who, my friend, has reason in his rage?
'The ruling Passion, be it what it will,
The ruling Passion conquers Reason still.'

Alexander Pope
Moral Essays, Epistle III

ONE

Darling Bernadette,

As you have forbidden me to talk to you I must write. Today, if I am lucky, I will see you but not touch you; follow but not meet you; love at a distance, shunned. *Amor vincit omnia.* Remember? That was the love for *God* which conquered everything. Your religion. Mine too now – in my way. For I have found that earthly love delivers no less. My love for you has conquered me. Its ferocity has led me to do things I would despise in others. It has overawed me with its turbulence, its banality, its power to twist my life around its lightest whim. The casualties of this passion are all about me and yet – I would not have it any different.

What others condemn as a waste of life I hold to as my time of crowning happiness. Even the grief is remembered with desire: the necessary thorn protecting my incomparable rose. Bernadette, black hair swaying across your eyes and mine, as you knelt above me, looked down, your slim oval face with the solemnity of a Madonna, and locked into me tightly, the wanton Magdalene, leaning your breasts onto me, erect nipples grazing on my hungry skin.

Amor vincit omnia does not only mean love for God but God's Love: in that case also I claim it. What else could it be that we had? Those moments when you closed your black eyes and murmured "Ssshhh . . . listen . . ." the sound of us together . . . my own eyes closed, joining you in our darkness which art heaven. And you opened your eyes for me to see the tiny speckles of dove grey flickering in the velvet-black pupils. Just below your right eye at the outside corner, placed there with perfect eighteenth-century delicacy, is the beauty spot you hated, eight similar markings on your upper left arm, five on your right, of varying sizes and textures; I could identify them all. "I love *that,*" you would say, "and I love *that . . .*" as you murmured our longing so feelingly. I had never known what it was to be loved before you. Where did you come from? Without you I would have missed the violent sensations of uncontrollable erotic love. You think I blame you, Bernadette. You too think I have shamed and ruined myself. No, no, no, no. To love and, even greater, to be loved. What better world is there? It fills the world. It *is* life. And your thin lascivious wicked mouth. I was free.

I will write to you to fill the days, to be near you, but most of all to try to cast a spell on you. I sit in this small room with its two electric bars, sagging single bed, a wardrobe whose doors are wedged with paper to keep them shut, and one cowpat-brown rug, knowing that less than half a mile away, across the town that saw us meet and love and break, *you* are there. Every night I try to will you – as I do now – to get up from your chair beside the fire, to walk to the door, to come down the long hill, on the narrow pavement, past the car park, through the two right-angled main streets of night-lit town, across the waste track to this shamble of railway terraced cottages where mine is the only one inhabited. You will open the door, that frown of uncertainty, and then perhaps, as sometimes happened, that wonderful smile – sly, provocative, generous, taunting, like your tongue – and we would be together again. Bernadette. I would be content to hold your hand: not even that, no, just to look at you. Could we once cast such spells? You bewitched me.

You were eighteen when we met: I was thirty-six years your senior. Even now, even here, I hesitate to put down my age in plain terms. Fifty-four. There. Still fearing the jibes at the foolishness of it all. But my love is foolish, even ridiculous – and it is also the sanest feeling I have ever known. It makes the world clear. It makes sense of what we have. Everything else – yes even the death, even that – is outside the flame that fed itself. With you I lived inside that flame and now I feed it at every moment. You can have no idea what you mean to me. I brood over our meetings – sometimes I made notes immediately afterwards: I know you won't like that, but this is a confession as much as a letter – and my second ambition is to remember them in such absorbing detail that they will fill out real time. So that I can spend a whole evening being with you in my imagination as once I was in reality. In doing that I could fill up the days and nights forever with no chinks for the needles of regret and anguish and pitiless self-blame. I am far from that perfection but I persevere.

So, darling Bernadette, whom even in a letter I dare not call *my* darling Bernadette, I will tell you, as briefly as I can, my story of our life. That which you know you will recognise to be true; as a consequence, I hope that you will believe that which you do not know, or perhaps did not choose to know. More a document than a letter, I suppose, but the only way I can write it is to address it to you. I like to think that one day you may read it.

A mouthful of whisky, a pause to lean back from this shaking cardtable with its cheap conical lamp which throws the shape of Mercator's globe onto the ceiling and I can edge back into our world – your slender shoulders, myself hard inside you, aching but holding, wanting you and praying that time would freeze, the subversive grey speckles betraying your solemn gaze, for you would open – that mouth – laugh at my reverence, snap your teeth and attack! And the new almost mystic feeling afterwards, not in my heart, not abstract, but deep in the pit of my gut, that everything, everything, was good. Where did that come from?

TWO

"I think we should give it to the Kennedy girl," I said.

My two fellow judges were not happy.

"It's the best essay. She is the right age. She is from the town."

"She's certainly from the town," Christopher said, sarcastically.

"My problem exactly." Frank, the eternal seconder.

"An image problem."

"Whether we like it or not this will reflect not only on us but on Rotary."

"An image problem," Christopher repeated, sucking on a pipe. He was the only man I knew who still sucked one of those large curved Sherlock Holmes jaw-straining pipes, and he sucked on it knowingly. "It comes down to standards. What we stand for."

"That's the crux, I'm afraid," Frank agreed. "And it's nothing to do with discrimination." Wrong again, small-town snobberies terrorised his life.

"The girl herself," sucked Christopher, fat, perhaps on the wind he had sucked into himself over the years through the wide crater bowl of that bloodhound pipe, "may be all well and good."

"I'm sure she is," said Frank, at his most Christian: a sidesman; an Anglican.

Was I as angry with them then as now? I do believe I was.

"It is not only the best essay," I repeated. "Bernadette Kennedy has submitted the only essay which is literate, entertaining and now and then, even funny. There is no contest."

"Ah, but is it *about* a contest?" Christopher peered up at my advantage of about five inches with his best owlish, Poirot twinkle.

"We held a competition."

"But *did* we?" he ruminated visibly, jaws munching around the walking stick of a stem. *"Did* we?"

Thank God, I remember thinking, presumably then and on so many similar occasions at that time, for early retirement. In a month I would be free and under that pretext all the scheduled boredom of my bank manager's necessary public relations could be re-evaluated: i.e. dumped.

To his credit, Anglican Frank was uncomfortable with Christopher's Jesuitical development.

"It *was* a competition, Christopher. We can't deny that."

"I wasn't denying it. I was testing it."

Christopher is a solicitor, but on such occasions he dreams of being a great barrister teasing juries with his eloquence, outwitting Counsel for the Defence, indulgently playing along the Judge.

"You are the Chairman," Frank said to me, looking at his watch for the fourth or fifth time. "I'm really supposed to be in bed by now. I told Sarah I'd be home before nine." I knew Sarah and I sympathised. "And you're the one who knows about books."

"We all have an equal vote." Christopher took out the pipe to deliver what was clearly a reprimand.

Frank flushed a little C. of E. flush and my hand was strengthened.

"But he is a writer," Frank persisted. "That makes a difference."

So. My occasional articles for the *Cumberland News* and *Cumbria* had not been in vain! I could be called 'a writer'. I accepted the flattery without flinching. An interest in all aspects of the Lake District – which had begun as no more than a watertight excuse to get me out of the house without guilt or hindrance – had surprised me by growing into a demanding hobby. The published pieces were all the proofs my wife ever needed.

"A writer," said Christopher, now beating the air with the pipe, "is not necessarily the best judge of writing. Not neces-

sarily." All five syllables were heavily beaten out for the gentle-
men of the jury.

Frank looked again at his watch and made his decision. "It's
beyond me," he said. "It's just a prize. I have to get up in the
morning so I'm off in five minutes flat." He meant it. And that
is why he runs the best fruit and vegetable shop for miles around.

"What about the position of Rotary in all of this?"

Frank would not be drawn. I took my cue.

"We asked for essays of three to four thousand words on any
aspect of life in the town. Ages seventeen or eighteen next
birthday. Must have lived here for at least six years. Prize
£350 to be spent preferably on books or foreign travel. And
Bernadette Kennedy –"

"The Kennedys will drink it away," said Christopher, coming
clean at last. "Every penny."

He had a point. Be fair. Of all the families at the rough end of
town, Roman Catholic, touch of Irish, gambling, loudness,
weekend fighting, petty thieving, gaol and dole and drink, the
Kennedys took the palm.

"And where is she going?" The advocate struck again. "Nowhere! Leaving school! At least four of the others are off
to college. They will be a fine advertisement for Rotary.
The Kennedy girl will end up in the pubs with the rest of
her family and the £350 and Rotary will become a laughing
stock."

"You can't tar her with the family brush," I said. "Agreed,
Frank?"

He nodded, far from wholly convinced but by now desperate
to get this foreign matter which served no purpose and made
no profit over and done with.

"Innocent until proven guilty," I said to Christopher – rather
obviously, I thought – but to my delight the casual jibe stopped
him.

"Two minutes," said Frank.

"What if she ends up on Social Security?"

"Our job was to judge the twenty-six essays. Hers was the
best."

"Near the knuckle now and then," said Frank, unexpectedly,
and suddenly he grinned. "Remember that bit about our vicar

and that drunk blonde what's her name? She got them both to a 'T'."

"That was supposed to be a story," said Christopher, a touch desperately, "so she maintained, but was it or wasn't it?"

"All that's beyond me. Time's up. I'm off."

"We need your vote. It is highly unconstitutional to walk out of a meeting like this without fulfilling your responsibility." Christopher jabbed out his pipe like Exhibit A. "Unconstitutional *and* improper."

Once again Frank flushed. But this time it was the angry flush of an honest small businessman accused of fiddling.

"My vote goes to the Kennedy lass. That settle it?"

"It does."

"Constitutional enough for you?"

"Certainly," I replied.

"Then I'll bid you both a very good night." His cap was planted on his head with the finality of a full stop.

And thus, Bernadette, you got the prize.

Which did indeed – or most of it – as you told me much later – disappear down the throats of your proud family. Frank came to fewer meetings after that and now, I believe, he has resigned.

You were given the award at an occasion which managed to be both awkward and jolly. Your demure appearance and aspect of humble gratitude were noted with relief. Three months later I had to see you for your report on what you had done with the money. The report could be made verbally. You chose that method and came to my house on May 6 at 6 p.m. I had retired by that time and had just relished a solitary day on the Caldbeck Fells, vexed that I had to cut it short to see you. My wife was in bed ill as she so often was. I took you into the front room which rather fancifully I called my study – it *was* impressively congested with books – and I offered you a glass of sherry. You accepted.

Did I fall in love with you then? It was the first time we had been alone – and I clearly remember the unease I experienced. You were wearing the black blouse – which looked like silk – and the rather short tight tweed skirt. Although it was summer it was cold and you were wearing dark stockings – back in fashion you told me later. You sat in one of the deep armchairs and crossed your slim legs and there was an inch or two of that tantalising junction between the top of your stocking and the hem of your skirt. I have deliberated a great deal on why that particular sight should be so voluptuous. Is it to do with the thought that men see the last line of defence after which there is apparently no resistance, the way free to what we might call open country? Is it a seductive and primordial remnant of the sacrificially bound virgin? Or some inexplicable tactile excitement, material turning into skin? The historical sensuality of all alluring clothes? Or no more than an example of Pavlovian pornographic ruttishness brought on by a particular upbringing in a particular time? Or was it a promise? – nothing accidental about the crossing of the legs, a demure but promiscuous invitation – you were capable of all that, thank God. Just a larky uncomplicated little tease. Yet although I was affected by the unexpected indication of your sexuality, I do not think I fell in love at that moment. I was alerted – as you see I remember it very clearly: but not yet bewitched; the beginning of the beginning perhaps.

Your hair: I must not forget your hair which swept and entwined about your Modigliani face and was later plaited about me in ways to make a Casanova choke with envy. Glossily framing your features, it rested below your shoulders in a long wave, its darkness and the gloom of the east-facing study giving a deliquescent shimmer to your eyes. I wondered then and have done since whether there was not some gypsy blood in you. There used to be a regular Romany camp in winter around the town – the local dialect is pimpled with Romany. You were that or a Celt: something exotic but not alien to this mongrel settlement in the far north where Celts, Britons, Romans, Norsemen, Normans, and no doubt a fair sprinkling of nomads have fed the local species.

I like my little learning. Perhaps I was over-anxious to pass it on to you. You were impressed, genuinely I think, when I showed you my collection of books on the Lake District, the few first editions: Hutchinson, Otley, Gilpin, West – and decent selections of the Wordsworths, Coleridge, De Quincey – I had surprised myself by taking an interest in them, through their Lake District connection of course – and all the time I was

showing the books to you I was wondering which one I could
give you. It had to be one which I could only just afford to lose
– I was not in love with you – or I did not realise it – but even
then I knew that it had to have real value to me. I chose the
small leather-bound edition of W. G. Collingwood, with the maps
neatly folded into a special pouch at the side. That delighted
you, didn't it? "Just like a wallet," you said.

You had sipped at the sherry but left most of it. Later of
course I learned that you hated sherry. I only noticed that you
had left it long after you had gone and I was drawn back to the
study, back into the atmosphere of your absence. At the time I
was so taken with showing off that I observed nothing. For I
sensed your eagerness, your openness, *you*. From that evening
on, the study was transformed. I would go to it to taste what I
later realised was the memory of that hour of innocence, that
casual passage between myself as the new-born tutor, you the
student, both of us playing our parts. For I was and am no more
than a retired bank manager in his mid-fifties with an interest
in local history brought on chiefly by a shameful need to have a
reason to get out of the house; you, alas, were never to be the
student you could, you should, you still ought to be. But I get
ahead of myself.

My wife called down. She wanted some tea. I felt embarrassed
that you should be there when I had to set about such a domestic
chore. Why was that? Was I already wanting to be seen as
manly? Did I know, so early, that in your culture such an act
would be regarded as rather 'soft'? Perhaps not: I have learned,
at last, not to generalise – as we all did at the judging – about
'the Kennedys', 'the rough end of town', 'them'. More likely I
was irritated because my wife disturbed what was unconsciously
gathering strength to become the greatest force in my life. But
I made the tea. Offered you a cup. You refused. I feared you
were impatient – you had a date with 'the gang', you told me,
later – and we had not had 'your report'.

Facing you, armchair to armchair, holding my teacup, I
listened while you lied. I never suspected you. You had drawn
out the money instantly, you said, and spent half of it on books.
You were keeping the other half – rather more than half, you
corrected yourself (very clever, very plausible) as the basis for

savings you intended to make for a trip abroad. You had never been abroad. Paris. The galleries, the Left Bank, the Louvre, Notre Dame and that new building with all its insides on the outside. 'O' Level French.

It was not an unmitigated lie. You had indeed bought half a dozen books – mostly paperbacks; you did, you do, dream of going to Paris, and perhaps you were saving for it. But the bulk of the Rotary Prize Money had been flushed down the gullets of the Kennedys and friends on a Saturday night bash which had turned into a legendary riot. You betrayed none of that. I, of course, then deep in my stockaded middle-class segment of the town, may at the time have heard rumours of a local Bacchanalia but would not have connected them with you and certainly not with the upright and sober funds of Rotary. Like all English towns, we have our concentric circles which need never intersect. That was to be one of our problems and also part of the intoxication.

I was worried about the money which I assumed you still had. I explained the workings of the different accounts then available. I'm sure I suggested that you put it into a deposit account which yielded interest. You preferred to have the money to hand, you replied, calmly, and nailed it down by saying that you liked to get it out and look at it now and then! You had never seen so much cash in one bundle. I was charmed and I shooed away my anxiety about money not properly secured. At that time unless money was in an account earning maximum interest I thought it was delinquent. But your simple 'I like to look at it' disarmed me. I should have guessed then.

Suddenly you were gone. I made supper for Angela and took it up to her. Talked to her about the news of the day as I had done for years. We could talk for long stretches almost finishing each other's sentences – so habitual and worked on had this conversation become. It was one voice. It was also a substitute for real conversation. The alternative was to say virtually nothing at all which would have been too unfair and sad. About twenty minutes made me feel useful. Perhaps other empty marriages are built on similar cultivated routines. It was a way of not talking and yet not admitting it.

I went back to my study to copy down my notes as I did after

every expedition, however trivial. It was a part of the day I
valued. Something romantic about it. The evening well gathered
in, curtains drawn, the handsome brass lamp like a beacon to
scholarship on the big schoolmaster's oak desk which Angela's
mother had left to me, books glowing on the shelves. I felt part
of a long tradition of writers in their cells or studies, opulent in
it, meagre practitioner though I was. A cup of coffee (decaffeinated in those virtuous days). Above all a feeling that by some
luck and reasonable management I had come to a time in my life
where I was sufficiently content and blindly complacent. One
married daughter – childless – in Australia. Angela upstairs with
a book and sometimes the murmur of the radio. That lurid
orange bedjacket would be sprinkled with crumbs, splashed with
ash. But I was alone at the desk, peering at the scribbled notes
before tapping them into neat black lines on new white sheets.
Nothing else mattered. And then the cat came and sat in the
armchair, your armchair, as she does so often.

I noticed your sherry glass. Hardly touched. I did something
which surprised me for at that time I was no drinker. Instead of
pouring it back into the bottle, I drank it. Did I think – my lips
are now where her lips were so recently? I recalled your saying
you liked to look at the money and I made a note of that remark
on a new sheet of paper.

THREE

Dear Bernadette,

I'm sorry, sorry, sorry. You have to believe it was an accident. Will you believe me? You must. I have stuck to my promises to the letter. And the spirit. Don't try to catch me out. I am not protesting that it is hard or that you could seem to be cruel because it is my own choice. I would rather live here with the thought that occasionally I can glimpse you – *not spy on you* – above all be in the same place as you are. I won't go on. We agreed I wouldn't meet you. Sorry. Finis.

But this morning *was* an accident. You know I go up the street to buy my paper. I could have it delivered but, pathetically, I find it a useful lure to make me get up and out in the morning. You know how keen I am on my papers: you once called me a 'newsprint junkie'. So that was why I was outside Reay's. I knew you would meet Theresa in her lunch break at 12.30 and I make sure that I am nowhere near the High Street at that time. Be fair.

Last night I slept hardly at all. I am trying to write something and that is difficult enough. What complicates it, though, is that even when I am *not* writing, *especially* when I am not writing, the business goes on and on inside my head. I keep thinking of what I have missed out, of how I can express the feeling behind it all. You called me an 'old worrier'. You were right. And so I sleep badly: last night I slept even worse than usual. Excuses? Yes. For some matters there are excuses. You need not have looked at me as if I had struck an innocent child. You need not have turned away your head and cut me with an expression which seemed to express violent distaste. Oh Bernadette, do all the other times mean nothing to you at all? Is all the meaning of past pleasure spent?

So I got up late, I hovered over my notes, dabbed a better (or was it?) adjective here, culled sentences there. I have really come to enjoy going over it again with my thesaurus, double checking it like the accounts. Then went out. It is not easy these days. Apart from everything else I look terrible – was it the grey in the beard that made you turn your head away so very sharply, or the general uncombed look? I keep reminding myself to get a haircut, to do something about my clothes and so on *in case* I bump into you. I should have done it. You were right to turn away. What can a ravishing, subtle, quicksilver young woman at the outset of her life conceivably find attractive in a grey and wild-eyed loon? Attractive? You must find me repugnant. Who could blame you? But the rule was that I never *would* see you again. Now I seem to have broken it.

It was, please understand this, not by design. I wanted to hurry up the street – which is no more than I usually do, as most people are embarrassed to see me. But a small number are loyal and Miss Wallace as usual and Frank – always a conscientious 'Hello' – and then Joe Barnes went out of his way to stop me on the street and chat. It was kind of him. I could not rebuke his generosity by rushing on and so, although I fretted, I stayed. By the time I got to Reay's it was almost 12.30, but how was I to know that you had arranged to meet Theresa outside that precise shop at that time? There was a queue and Brian was on his own and more minutes passed by. That is all.

When I came out at last, there you were.

Oh, Bernadette, there you were. However much you punish me for this, I have seen you again, full face, broad daylight. Was there just an instant – before you turned away – just the fraction of a moment when you looked at me with something less than dismay? Was that your instinctive reaction, too soon superseded by the bitter recollection of my shameful behaviour? As I study that meeting more closely, I am encouraged. There *was*, I am certain, something in your first look which was caring. Even loving. I felt it then – lightly, but it was there. Now that I remember and examine it scrupulously, I am certain. You still have some feeling for me – some love?

Can I *will* it to you? Can I somehow inhabit your mind so that you too think of this morning and seek out the truth of that very first moment? I began by saying I was sorry. I'm not at all sorry. I've seen you, been a few feet away from you, looked at you full in the face – you have stopped looking too thin: good – and I have more hope than I have had for weeks. Don't send me a note telling me I have broken my word and must go. You can't do that. Theresa's unfeeling laugh will stop you doing that because although she is your sister you will very likely have felt that the laugh was unfair on me however much you may despise me. Yes. I can stay. But I can't send this letter. Do you know what it is like to have your love forever forbidden – cries in a deserted room, words on a dumb tongue . . . *But I saw you!*

FOUR

I think I have found it. So many moments – and so few – since we met. To isolate that particular beat of time and give it the attention it deserves took considerable organisation. That, though, has always come quite easily to me. I have my diary, my notes and, despite the whisky, quite a good memory. Perhaps because of the whisky. Although I am a little woozy on some days I am nothing like as bad as I was during the mad spell. And I can stop drinking for a day or two if I feel I need to. There is undoubtedly an easier flow in my mind from one association to another when I have had a few mouthfuls of scotch or better still – for treats, that is to say, on desperate days – malt whisky. It doesn't pay to write at the time or even to read – but it helps me to be better company to myself. I can sit in front of those electric bars and persuade myself that although I have not the Great Thing in my life I am as content as could be hoped for without it. The music has not all gone.

Of course if I had you beside me, then life would be – as for some (I have their number) days it was – unimaginably whole. Next to you there is so very little. This condemned terraced cottage reflects that. There is something serious about this cheap drab place and it helps. With the whisky.

I am amused at the song and dance they make about alcohol these days. They have a point. But I remember someone on a television programme reeling off the names of great artists who had taken their drop; and I look around the town and see those who drink and take life by the neck, as often as not they are no worse and usually more fun than the others. As if I needed any excuse but you. Yet you are not an excuse at all. Rather the drinking was also part of the revelation of what a life was – a revelation brought to me by you.

Now I have the very moment it began. Trapped it like a butterfly between cupped palms, fluttering wildly but trapped. Tuesday May 16 a minute – certainly no more – before 7 p.m. Perhaps I can prompt you to remember? To trace it back to its source might renew that source in you. You might remember when it was clear, fresh, auspicious, and that could wash away all the later sins and stupidities. Your religion ought to have trained you in the habit and even though you no longer practise it, your Roman Catholicism is still deeply part of you. I always saw that. Misguidedly, I told you that.

So, on 16.5.89 at 18.59; outside Christopher's office where I had enjoyed the pleasant task of updating my will. Partly through his continuing guilt at offending Frank and annoying me over the award to you – whom he had subsequently employed(!) – this had been followed by a couple of glasses of celebratory sherry. I'm sure he put it on my bill.

The High Street was empty when I came out of his office. The evening was slate-grey cool, the pubs would begin to fill up later, only on Saturday nights was there any throb of crowd in the centre of the town and that not at all friendly to my generation. I turned left to go back home. Walked (I have re-enacted it) six or seven paces and then all but crashed into you as you flung yourself out of the door of The Crown.

You were laughing violently at something that had happened inside the pub. You were by no means drunk but you had enjoyed 'a couple' at what had been the end of a belated leaving-party for the girl in the office whose job you had taken. When you saw me you came to an abrupt exaggerated arrest of solemnity and then, unable to hold it, *you fell against me* with forcefully renewed laughter. *You yielded yourself against me.* I felt those perfect firm, but pliant breasts softly on my chest. For an instant your head was on my left shoulder and your hair pillowed against my neck and my cheek. I sensed the slenderness of your arm as you – again for a mere instant – clung to me as the last tremor of laughter shivered through you. And your hips closed against mine. I felt – and I *know* I felt it in those seconds – I felt you move towards me more than the circumstances warranted. Unless I am badly mistaken you pressed your hips – be clear! –

your groin against mine; for a whisker of time only but – provocatively.

It was as if a bonfire which had been built up without my being aware of it were suddenly ignited. The flame leapt up. Heavens opened. You moved away.

"Oh God!" You were still gasping a little from the laughter. "Sorry! She's so *funny*, Maureen. Sorry."

"That's all right."

"You of all people," you said and St Mary's clock struck seven, which seemed the seal to my bewildering new state.

You stood back as if to examine me. Perhaps it was then – although it could have been later – that I noticed what you were wearing. Exactly the same as when you had come to my home. I did not realise how very limited your wardrobe was. Angela – my only other experience – has a wardrobe full of clothes although she never goes anywhere. I could wish you had always worn that outfit. I would have bought you a hundred replicas.

"Going home?"

"Yes," I must have said.

"I'll walk with you," you said. "I'm calling on a friend that way."

So we set off through the empty town, past St Mary's Church, Fox's, butcher's, the unisex hairdresser, the new children's clothes shop, already in that short distance out of the shopping centre of the place: five thousand souls and not one abroad, for which I was profoundly thankful. Because I was in a turmoil. Astonishment, freedom, utter lightheadedness, shyness, crazy intoxication, energy, anxiety, exhilaration, already missing you although you were walking beside me – chatting away about the leaving-party, about your new job in the office (I did not realise then that you were the first in your family ever to achieve an office job) – already wanting you although your youth and promise seemed utterly unattainable, wanting you that moment with an intensity I feared you had to notice. But you chattered on. "I noticed you were rather quiet," you said when we talked about it. "But I thought you were that type."

I was instantly 'In Love'. Conflagration confirmed. The flame roaring away, all the clichés and banalities burning and mocking on the pyre. Yes – it *is* like this. Makes your knees go weak.

Makes you dizzy. Makes you want to do foolish things. Makes
you search for the songs of the psalmist and all the singers since.
"Well, I leave you here," you said and smiled. The smile that
cuts to the nerve. "See you." Those were your last words. I
noted them down. I cannot believe they were coldly casual or
merely a habit. "See you," you said and meant it? Hoped for it?
Your eyes were brilliant with fun when you looked at me, the
grey shards glittering. I watched you walk away as long as I
plausibly could and then walked slowly along to our impressive
sandstone double-fronted Victorian detached house in one acre
of garden. I was a man transformed, at once the same man and
someone essentially and wholly different from he who had set
out from the place on town errands a few hours before. I realised
that I had been an emotional bankrupt. Quite suddenly I was
not just solvent but affluent, loaded. Transformed. Could not
everybody see it? How could I possibly disguise it from Angela?
Look – I was someone else as surely as if a full moon had turned
me into a werewolf. At last I knew what it was. This simple
and so damagingly overused word appeared like a physical
phenomenon – a coral reef of the mind, a mountain completely
unknown until now. Absurd? Yes. Exaggerated? No. *True*. I
had been stunned by love.

Did it really happen as a *coup de foudre*? When I was rummaging
around the literature of love I came across that phrase and it
seemed so true. It is rather embarrassing to admit to – very
un-English – a French phrase to rub it in – but truly it was some
kind of blow I felt at that moment. It must have been a most
powerful intimation of the luminous satisfaction of need, of
lust, which dawned in me when you pressed – so sweetly, so
unexpectedly – your thighs against mine. Instinct is the fastest
thought and takes longest to unravel. But I knew. Even though
I had never experienced the wildness, the tender, wanton,
exhausting sex which there was to be between us, my intuition
knew it, my imagination responded.

I assure you that I have gone over those moments time and
time again. I am used to being careful, to checking lists and
scanning accounts. I enjoy my thoroughness – it was the consolation of a boring job. All that I have described did indeed happen

before the stroke of seven. Later meetings compacted the feeling; deepened it and tested it. The neatness of hindsight is always a threat to the messiness of the real moment – but I am as sure as I can be that there was a moment in my life when I did fall in love, when the heavens did open, when, if I squeeze the memory as hard as I can, there was a feeling of helpless, emotional vertigo.

Once upon a time when I could not sleep I used to count up the money and investments that Angela and I had. Value the house, the pensions, the money market, know to a decimal point the worth of the shares and gilts, calculate the growth of the pension fund, know to a pound what was in the various accounts: and then luxuriate in comparisons (I had their figures too, most of them) with my acquaintances in the town. Now when I cannot sleep I return to that moment. You tumbling out of the pub. The very pitch and volume of your laugh. Your thighs against mine. The church clock marking my fate. Seven.

FIVE

The next morning – I made a note – I woke up with a lift of excitement. It took me some time to identify it. There was considerable pleasure in tracking down the precise quality of the excitement. I can remember a similar scent of the hunt when, in the old days, doing it without a calculator, I sniffed a crucial error in a vital and complex pattern of figures and knew that by the patient deployment of simple rules, I would winkle it out.

This new excitement, when I identified it finally, was to do with holidays and sex. More specifically those childhood holidays when I woke up in a boarding-house on the sea-front besotted with the idea of the sea and the sand, and deeply secure in the conviction that I would love it all, all the day long. The day was wrapped up and every removal of a layer of covering would reveal more tempting pleasures. And the sex? Specifically, one girl with whom I had my most successful sexual experiences which, though not the first, was quite early on, thank goodness, because it gave me the chance to get an understanding of what I would have with you. Perhaps without her I would not have had the gleam of an idea of what lay in wait. For about three weeks, with her, I woke up with a stirring of sexual anticipation. Excitement, childhood holidays, good sex – already you promised all that and we had not even held hands!

I made a point of seeing you on the street that afternoon. It was easy to organise. You waved but looked a touch suspicious. Later you told me that you thought I was checking up on you: that I had heard how the money had been spent and was seeking a moment to challenge you about it. I interpreted your look as a mild accusation or an instance of what I came to know as your worrying intuition. I thought that you resented me in some way or, much worse, read my thoughts. I was unprepared for you to do that; the strategy had not been developed. The 'strategy' at that stage was an excuse for inaction.

I began to plan it that evening in my study, inspired by the chair in which you had sat. I discovered in time that by concentrating hard enough I could all but conjure you back into that chair. Not only was I able to repossess that moment, I was able to enjoy the added charge built up through the subsequent encounters. I was already learning the art of recollecting and layering and thus intensifying passion.

By the time I had finished the strategy paper it looked rather like one of the annual projections I used to do at the bank. Months divided into weeks along the bottom line; on the left hand vertical, the progress I hoped to make; starting with Another Private Conversation, preferably in this room. How offensive it seems now – but you must remember my loneliness and my ignorance: and my shamefully schoolboyish class-raddled and crass behaviour. Needless to say I put it in code although Angela had not been in my study for about five years.

This absurd activity gave me the purest happiness I had known for years – and – ridiculously – it was underpinned by the certainty of our inevitable union. For that moment I was in perfect control. The curious thing is that any of it worked out at all as I predicted. Occasionally, when I check back, there is an accidental accuracy now rather sad. For none of it mattered. But during those warm evening hours with my word processor and cups of decaffeinated, I was the happy man. Perhaps turning love into theory is as happy as someone like me could, then, reliably get. I remember hearing on the radio that musicians and mathematicians shared a similar faculty and it could give them an unusual degree of contentment. We footsoldiers in the art of numbers might be a second cousin to that. In the end, though, it was just a way of convincing myself I was in contact with you.

So I began my own humble mathematics. Stage One, I wrote: *Prepare the Ground*. Stage Two would be the *First Advance*; Stage Three the *Full Pursuit*; Stage Four *The Conquest*, the wish to further the deed. I wanted there to be seven stages – seven having more significance as a number – it echoed the clock; and besides, I liked rather longer lists. Four seemed too brisk. Looking back now I see that I tried to pad it out by putting sub-headings under the main headings. Under *Preparing the Ground*, for instance, I put (a) find out about her family (b) find out about her work (c) find out about her friends (d) dig into the background history. (d) was desperation. But I needed a fourth point to make the page look balanced. Four headings each with four sub-sections had a purposeful look about it – or so I thought in those early days when the disciplines of banking were turned to surprisingly useful ends. (Oddly, although (d) was set down for reasons of symmetry rather than sense, it proved something of a runner.)

Most of all, though, I look at that list now – as I am doing under the bare light of my bulb, yellow as a full moon – and think: who was he? Who was this man creaking towards the middle of his sixth decade who thought he could lay down such a repulsive plan of campaign which took into account nothing of importance? Nothing of your character – unknown; nothing of my own – which would necessarily be changed by the execution of the plan. Yet on he sailed, the retired bank manager with the invalid wife and the interest in all things Lakeland, with charts as neat as monthly statements.

To my shame I have discovered yet another set of lists which bore the twin headings: GAINS: LOSSES: and a line down the middle of the page between them. I have sworn to tell nothing but the truth yet my adolescent exercise embarrasses me even more than some of the more erotic, humiliating and distressing confessions to come. But here it is: let me at least update it with today's comments which ought to be graffiti, necessary subtractions.

GAINS:

(a) rediscovery of the emotion of love (*How pompous!*)
(b) excitement in
    (i) the adventure (*Asinine!*)
    (ii) the consequent deceits (*Utterly disgraceful to think of this as a gain – a monstrous smugness.*)
(c) the interest of an uncharacteristic act i.e. who will I

turn out to be?!! (*At the time I must have considered that to be so slight or amusing that it deserved the jocularity of two exclamation marks – now it seems the only one of the slightest relevance.*)

LOSSES:

(a) it is a foolish action – and a banal one – older (old) man, young woman (girl), ridicule must follow
(b) probable hurt to Angela (*Unforgivable, who was I then?*)
(c) possible disruption of a hard earned routine (*Oh God!*)

'Possible'! 'Probable'! I was asking for it and I got it. What sort of bland, blind creature was I – and yet a respected and even well-liked man? What an accounting there has been since. Mockery and disorder. Mayhem and darkness. Revenge!

There is another way to look at it. I was *so* intoxicated, so toppled from the perch I occupied that at first I sought refuge in what I knew. I was a man of lists. They now came to my aid to absorb, perhaps even to divert the all but overwhelming FACT. You.

Or they could have been my first love letter. The love letter of a man still cemented in his banks of sad and compromised certainties. I've learned that many of us write when in one extremity or another – even if it is only a letter, a note to ourselves instantly destroyed, a coded diary piece, an emotional attempt at poetry. Lists were what I reached out for when I needed to staunch the time before I next saw you. There you were – laid out so neatly. I look at them now – the crass battalions of confidence, and start by laughing, end by grieving. All vanquished. Losses still mounting. New lists waiting to be drawn up. This document/letter is anti-lists. It wants to be a spell.

"Sherry?"

"No thanks."

I could not assume that you did not drink. The touch of alcohol on your breath was part of my complete recollection of your stumbling out of the pub.

"You don't like sherry?"

"Hate it."

You smiled. Even at my age I would have found it difficult to admit anything so openly in those few self-conscious little 'parties' we late middle-aged, late converts to timid good living would lay on for each other. 'Hate it' told me: bold, even reckless. The smile said 'Forgive me' and 'I'll charm you'.

The first lines of the first sketch were drawn.

"I have some whisky."

"It doesn't matter."

"And gin. I'm not sure about tonic."

"Really, it doesn't matter." You smiled again, this time challengingly, saying 'Take me as I am'. "I'll be going out to the pub later anyway."

"Do you go to the pub very often?"

"All the Kennedys drink. Everybody knows that."

I noted soon after you left that you said that with 'a certain weariness'.

You were nervous. You thought you had been found out about the prize money.

"Please sit down." I indicated 'your' chair – although you had sat in it only once. You avoided it and, to my immediate disappointment, sat on a hard-backed chair. You crossed your legs and kicked the overhanging leg, impatient, I suspected at the time, to be gone. Your face dark against the sunlight. Your hair dangling idly over your face.

You were wearing tight-fitting light-blue jeans, freshly washed, I'd guess, a 'matelot' top – horizontal white and blue stripes; a thin brick-red plastic belt and bright red shoes. I thought – if it is possible to think retrospectively simultaneously with thinking actually – I might have thought that I would have preferred you as you had been before: more formal, more feminine, more old-fashionedly alluring. But I loved the way you looked. One shoulder of your matelot shirt slipped away; and that tender rather bony shoulder became the focus of my attention. Not that I gazed at it all the time; I discovered an ocular shyness in myself. But it was your left shoulder I worshipped in that second encounter in my house.

'Why am I here?' Your whole attitude expressed that emphatic query. Your very shape and posture could be read as a question mark.

"I suppose you wonder why I dropped a note asking you to pop along this evening."

You froze. Cataleptic. The reaction was so quick and so fierce. All the gentility and padded ease of the room fled, as if a stoat had landed in a chicken coop or a street fighter had walked into a nicely, nicely saloon bar. You looked at me with a defensive intensity which held an element of malevolence. I felt – I noted it – a chill, an unmistakable ripple of goose pimples. You were magnificent and you said not a word.

"I wondered," I stumbled into apologetic speech. I felt sick in my stomach. I must not scare you off, that was my hammering panic. "Your History teacher – I talked to Mr Skelley – he's in Rotary – he said you were one of the most promising pupils he had ever taught. That was his phrase. He was very disappointed when you decided to leave before finishing your studies."

Still you said nothing. You supposed, I now realise, that I had sniffed around to build up a case against you. Oh! The neat and synthesised plans! Oh, those charts and tight dates and careful subdivisions! What help were you now? Please don't walk out, was all that I was thinking. *Please stay*.

"And I talked to one or two others," I went on, helplessly, stepping deeper into the mire; you detested being talked about in any context. "All of them speak very highly of you. Very. You could have got into a good university. Mr Skelley mentioned Oxbridge. But you chose to leave."

By now either my manner or what I said reassured you and just as suddenly you relaxed. The room filled out once more with my own friendly spirits.

"I should have left earlier," you said.

"Why?"

"That stuff's not for me. It never was."

"Why not?"

You shook your head; lips tight, almost pursed. That was all

my answer. I did not know how to take the conversation forward
and, not for the last time, you had pity on me.

"So you want to give me some sort of second chance."

You hit my ploy, bull's eye.

I muttered about needing someone to type up my articles,
help with the filing, come on the occasional field trip. It would
be a great help to me – of course I would pay – and it was
strictly part-time – an evening here, a Saturday morning or
afternoon there, a lecture, a Sunday outing into the Lake
District now and then . . . You let me stew but even as my head
sank and my voice dropped I saw the gentle, was it deceitful?
smile – which I adored – of the winning schoolgirl soften across
your lovely face . . . And I had reread your prize-winning story,
I said, very impressive, with a talent like that you should . . .

"You're on," you said.

'You're on.' Has such a bare sentence ever given so much
hope? The moment you left I rushed to my notebook dizzy with
the possibilities of love. 'You're on!'

I did not see you for two days after that. I will always believe
you avoided me deliberately. I went down into the town at times
guaranteed to cross your path but you eluded me. However
much you later protested, I know that it was on purpose. And
– as this is to be an honest document – I think that you did it to
provoke and inflame me. Some of this may have been unconscious on your part. At that juncture you were not the torrentially
self-aware woman you became. There was still a touch of the
schoolgirl in those early days; although you came to resent the
years sixteen to eighteen spent in education, you had been
marked by it and the charming, giggly, unknowing but cruel
games of schoolchildren were still, just, a part of you. So you
gave me the slip to torment me.

You succeeded. I saw myself as a misguided fool. 'You're on.'
The phrase which had become an instant talisman turned to
mockery. A quick get out, an ironic exit line, a mere tease, or,
most likely I thought, signifying nothing at all – just a couple of
syllables to conclude a conversation. In those two days I veered
between rage and despair. 'Never to see you again!' (what
non-punishment for you?) battled against 'Never to see you
again?' (what certain pain for me).

I have those moments still, although I try not to acknowledge them. Black mornings, black nights, seized by the panic of understanding that I will never be with you again for the rest of my life. There will be no more wild couplings, no more kissing as if truth depended on the strength and meaning of it, no more sex of a tenderness and ferocity to stop imagination, no more of those hundred and one serendipities of trivial mutual life through a long day – such days. Sailing across the hours feeling every minute fathoms deep in the fact of our being together. Now such parched shallow days, stumbling fretfully, racked by the minute. Only when I write this or take another thrifty drink at my one bottle a day (sometimes I cheat): only when I can uncover the past and climb into it . . . am I . . . numb? Anaesthetised? I should have been an archaeologist. I am an archaeologist. You are my seven cities of T⁀ny. It is 5.10 a.m. and I am weighed down by love for you. I know I will have to carry its granite weight for the rest of my life. And I want to: it is the best of life I can have. But I am tired now, Bernadette. The last drop. Cheers . . .

On the third day I did see you and you behaved like a terrible flirt. You were with Theresa outside Middleham the butcher's across from the fountain where the High Street makes a smart right-angled turn into King Street. You saw me coming – AND YOU LAUGHED AND RAN AWAY. *Ran* – around the corner. I felt hit. I looked around – for help? Or to make sure that no-one had noticed my humiliation? Absurd. The passers-by on the streets of the small Northern town were going about their own business and besides who then knew my feelings for you? Why did I think (a) that anyone *knew*? and (b) that anyone cared? All I had done – so far – was to ask you to be a part-time assistant – extending a friendly hand to a working-class (very) girl to help her continue her education. And to add to that pot of growing gold for Paris! I was safe. I ran towards the corner.

You had disappeared. *I was stymied.*

The town had been cross-hatched with back alleys until progress and planning scooped some of the heart out of it; but still the arches remained leading to twisting medieval lanes or the clear reminders of seventeenth-century pathways as well as to a car park and the new site for light industry. You could have taken any one of them. It was the lunch hour and a market day and the town was busy. I remember looking intently in Middleham's at the bloody carcasses and lumps of black pudding, the chops with a white plastic price tag stuck in them and the intestinally sinister coils of the famous local sausage and telling myself to remember my dignity. Furious just to catch a glimpse. Witch!

The only way I could possibly catch you was to trawl through all those aborted alleyways. So I trawled through them. I could always say, I thought, if challenged, that I was doing some field work on town history. Indeed I took out my diary and my pen and paused every now and then to look intelligently at a building and make a note! Like a small yacht facing a big wind, I tacked to and fro across the street, up and down the wriggling centre of the town: in vain. Twice I was sure I heard your laughter and two pairs of feet scuffle and run away. Of course you know the layout of the place so much better than I do. Too late I thought of going into a pub. I suppose it never occurred to me that you would go into a pub at lunchtime. An eighteen-year-old. A demure prize-winner. A newly fledged clerk. A prematurely retired scholar of 'exceptional promise'. But you were a vaga-bond, with Border and tinker stock, Romany even. A Kennedy. I walked home sick to my stomach and wrote you that first angry note.

You turned up, on the dot.

"You saw me and you ran away."
  "I didn't see you."
  "I don't believe you."
  "I'm off."
  "Look –"
  "I didn't come here to be called a liar."
  "Why did you come?"
  "I said I was interested in your offer."
  "You *must* have seen me."
  "Why? Were you waving a red flag?"
  "I saw you. And you laughed and ran away."
  "Why would I do that?"

"To – to –" I had worked out so many permutations that I was spoilt for choice but your denial made me hesitate.

"Come on. Why would I run away from you?"

Why indeed? I was, at that time, no more than a mildly surprising benefactor. A pillar of the town. Owning your time in the way that schoolteachers and your priest could own your time. You were obedient to me in exactly that unthinkingly dutiful way. My offer was to you no more than an extension of the Rotary prize. Why should you run away?

"I don't know." My reply was pathetic. Of course I knew! You were flirting. Of course I was right! And it was delicious – painful but innocent enough. But you always denied that. Now, of course, I am comforted. You wanted to hold on to the bond between us and feared that a lie would fray it to breaking. Once the lie was promoted so steadfastly – using all your considerable powers of sincere dissimulation – you were in too deep. Typically, you attacked.

"Who do you think I am, anyway?"

"I wasn't implying . . ."

"To behave like that. That's disgraceful. You must think I'm muck. My type. My family."

"Please. Bernadette. I was so sure."

"OK. But why did you come to the conclusion that I had run away?"

Oh clever Bernadette. You could always draw me back to the fire, the fire that burned me. I was on the spit of your indulgence now and you turned the handle slowly.

"I've told you, I don't know. Perhaps because I had been thinking about you."

"What had you been thinking about me? Not much by the sound of it."

"Since you left this room, I have been thinking about you all the time."

You looked around my study as if it were eavesdropping on this mumbled admission. You paused – did you pose pausing? – you made me aware beyond doubt that my words had penetrated and were logged.

"There's the fair at Carlisle tomorrow," you said. "Down on the Sands. Why don't we go?"

A fair! How deeply in my past was the memory of going with any pleasant anticipation to a fair. A career away, a class, or several gradations of class away, respectability away. Habits had been disciplined to direct me away from a childhood in which the arrival of the fair had been the thrill of the year. I had partly learned to mark my advance by my distance from such things.

To me now the fair was the bearpit, the cock-fighting ring, yobbo rampage, part of the British art of public vandalising. I had clambered out of that and become part of the new, late twentieth-century – 'we are all middle class now' – Britain, cultivating quiet but monied pleasures, inclining from the mass to the individual pursuit, discovering the rewards of things of the mind, putting the Goose Fair of loutish energy – however Falstaffian (Shakespearian yob), however fecund – well behind. The fair was the low beast expelled from my secure homeowning walls. I had worked hard to expel that beast. A fair was fear.

"I could meet you there," you said, kindly anticipating the rush of confusion which would be stirred up when I considered how to get there, how to engineer the lift I must offer you, where to pick you up, how to explain that (should explanation be necessary, as it would be) the lift could be the irreversible step. Was I ready for that?

As so often, your incisive intuition was remarkable.

"There's that Sands Centre. Where they have the concerts. I could meet you at the main entrance at about four. I'm going down to Carlisle to do some shopping anyway." Even in that last sentence there was generosity. You needn't think you are inconveniencing me, you were saying. But you did not relent on the invitation.

"The Sands was the place where they used to hold the public hangings," I said – why? God alone knows.

"That'll be all right then." The smile – your sweet one – head slightly lowered, eyes looking up, just the tips of the teeth seen, hair straying across your brow, expression gentle, unmocking. "See you if I see you. If you're busy – don't worry."

You left, but not before you almost moved to me to give me a kiss. You remember that? I will always regret it. Starchy me must have stiffened; but without reproach, you went away. Unkissed.

You had lied to me. You had made me feel guilty. You had forced a confession of devotion out of me far too soon in a context very unfavourable to me. You had sprung a test on me which was not insignificant. Come a fine day there would be hundreds, thousands at the fair, bound to be one or two who knew me – what *can* he be doing with that Kennedy girl?

You had taken control, although I would not yet admit it.

SIX

The first thing I noticed and the thing I noticed most all afternoon was about two hand-spans long. A black elasticated sort of woollen mini-skirt which stretched across your buttocks and your thighs like the peel on a tight apple. You had just bought it cheap in a sale, you said. A steal. It seemed to me that everyone else at the fair seemed no less transfixed by it. I know it was current fashion but, to me, only you were thus exposed. And, short as it wickedly was, it still rode up once or twice. It appeared to me that – hypertense as I was – you made only the most perfunctory of tugs to conceal the skimpy white lace – G-STRING! underneath. Everywhere we moved I sensed a rabble of lusting eyes swarming up your thighs. The lusts of a hundred young men gobbling up that firm tanned flesh – and I, inadequate in a new green anorak, somehow cast as the defender of your honour – the timid line between you and mass sexual assault. I experienced a terror I had not tasted for many, many years: the tang of nausea in the dry throat, scared to look anyone in the eye, the willing myself – *all the time* – not to shake – the longing, longing, longing for it all to be over.

You whooped around the fair like a cowboy in a rodeo. Bucked the Whiplash Waltzers, screamed on the Wall Of Death, crashed the dodgems, squandered on the fruit machines, and sang as the Big Wheel spun above the town like a magic hoop. Young men with tattooed arms gathered to stare and shuffled to follow; rifles crackled on the ranges; the ragged army of the new English mob pressed and flowed on a spot which had tested and quartered many such for more than eight hundred years. The dragon was moving in on you – the target, the dark angel, the epicentre of danger. And I in my well-pressed navy-blue corduroys a palpitating St George, a sale-price anorak my shield.

We left after forty-five minutes, you bearing a stick of candyfloss as big as a guardsman's beaver, me beginning to shake with relief as the last of the tattooed Furies dropped away and we reached the safety of my two-year-old red Volvo estate. But oh, those legs!

Did you take pity on me to leave after so short a time? Or was the whole point instant and extreme gratification spent like a firework? And did *they* take pity on me, the bare-chested young men blotchy with a few days' hot sun – thinking that I was your father and because of that keeping just to the other side of the line. Crude calls and coarse invitations there had been – plenty – but you had protected me. You smiled at them all and – twice – shot back such a gobful of abuse it dropped your tormentor in his tracks, derisive hoots from his pals – squashed.

"You didn't enjoy that, did you?"

We stood at either side of the car, talking across the roof. I wanted to get in and be safe. The noise of the fair was too near.

"I wish I could have done."

"Why?"

"I feel out of touch with all that."

"So what?"

"They were people having a good time. I couldn't join in because – I was scared of them, to tell you the truth."

"I'm impressed you can admit to it. I could see you were scared. But you didn't back off, did you?"

"No."

The strain worked through like delayed shock. I grew suddenly shaky and leaned on the burning roof.

"Are you all right?"

You moved around the front of the car and then you held me.

"You're shaking. You're really shaking. God, I'm a selfish bitch. Here."

You pressed me to you, your breasts, your thighs against me, your arms about me, your head on my shoulder, your hair richly there to graze in. You felt me come hard against you and you did not yield.

"I don't know what you must think of me," you said.

"Please." Please don't move, don't move. Please.

All I wanted from the world at that moment was for you

to stay exactly, precisely, oh so precisely, as you were. An old-fashioned word came to mind and I made a note to make a note. Bliss.

And you obeyed. You knew what I wanted and you gave it to me. You could do that and you did do that many and many a time. I became a slave to your gifts.

"I didn't realise," you said, eventually, gently moving away from me. "I thought it was a lark."

You looked puzzled and rather solemn. Madonna replaced Magdalene.

"I'll see you then."

You turned to walk away.

"Bernadette."

"You won't want to be seen in your car with me."

You were right. But you gave me no alternative. And there I stood, stiff with desire, still feeling your physical imprint.

"We could go for a drink. It's a lovely evening. To a country pub."

Again you looked at me carefully. Then you pointed to your mini-skirt and grinned.

"In this?" Oh yes, I thought, oh *yes*. But "Just a minute," you said. Out of the plastic bag which bore the name of the shop in which you had bought the succulent micro-skirt, you took your jeans, stepped into them, wriggled them up your thighs and rolled off the skirt, which you bundled into the bag, but not before I had caught a decisive look at your outrageously inadequate underwear.

I drove you into the Northern Fells to a pub called The Sun in Ireby and made a vow on the way that I would not tell you what Keats had written about the place. I did not then want to be the new Pygmalion. The saloon bar was empty at that early hour. You asked for a half of lager (in deference to my presumed gentility). I risked a bottle of Guinness after which I went on to orange juice, taking no risks with my driving licence.

And the risks and the licence with you?

You were the demure respectful schoolgirl. No one watching us (no one was) could have uncovered anything but a platonic and rather detached relationship between the bank manager (retd.) and the lass young enough to be his daughter. The fact

that the bank manager's groin was in a buckling thresh of sweet
agony and the modest schoolgirl was plotting her moves like
Rommel would not have been discernible. I caved in and talked
about Keats and the others who had turned the Lake District
into a literary monument. It proved a good choice. Your teachers
had not exaggerated. You knew your stuff and quite soon, but
quite firmly, found ground on which to outgun me. Was this
thoughtful young woman talking about Michael and eighteenth-century shepherds and how they were *much* worse off
than the Wordsworth hero, the same wanton, drunk with orgias-
tic fire, who had galvanised the predatory macho of an entire
fairground? It was, and it was wonderful. You *are* wonderful.
Nobody like you. So many different women and so young to be
so many. Where did you come from?

We went back by the high fell road and pulled up to watch the
sun spreading pastel pinks and mauves through the few gauze
clouds over the Western Fells. It deepened to furnace copper
– burning the pastels away – and you got out of the car and
walked some distance up the lonely hillside, your arms folded
across your breasts. Looking penitent – or was it a little chilly?

Like a kite tugged in by a string, like the victim of a hypnotist,
like a somnambulist, I followed where you led. You unzipped
my anorak and lay it down on the ground, placing it, I remember,
most fastidiously. Then you lay back on it, looked up to me, and
I, dry-throated, head spinning, in terror for the second time that
day, fell to my knees and feared to touch you.

I had to stop there. It was suffocating, Bernadette, the meaning
of that first time. I was so nervous, so clumsy, so afraid to 'get
it wrong', so aching to 'get it right', not knowing – worries flying
into my head like those arrows at Olivier's Agincourt – not
knowing so much about me, about you, about what either of us,
both of us, wanted, panting in want and panic and scarcely
touching you. And you? What did you do? You took my head
and cradled it; you put my mouth to your breasts; you touched
me back into life and guided me into you where you held me and
slowed me down and *taught* me; *you*, the child; *I*, the adult.
Taught me my first lesson in how to love you, to make love
with you, to stay and harden more and move more steadily,

rhythmically, passionately, and then quiet again. You uncovered a talent I had no notion that I possessed but that night, bare on the bare fellside, you found it and by the end I was above you, propped up on my arms, and you were truly, no dissimulation, as I truly was, in a thrash of not sex – love is the word, abuse it as you may – love. I could do it – with you, only you: and do it like *this*, like *this*. God – how did that come about? And for this *long* – never before, and what boasts to myself about myself ricocheted through my mind even the first time – and then, dark now, covered by rugs from the car, the second time ("Again please," you said, and drew me in). It was the end of me. You were the end of me that night, darling Bernadette. From that night on I was part of you and I will be until my life slips away like the copper sun.

I, thou, she, he, we, you, they.

I described that too briefly. I described that as I did it the first time. I want to be able to describe it like the second time when the earth did move and all the clichés of Romantic love roosted in me in you.

I shall try because it meant, it means so much to me. If I had to select one part out of my entire life to relive or to keep or to carry through the barrier to whatever may be beyond, I would choose those times when I was inside you. Nothing begins to compare with that. Then I was fullest alive – not 'just sex': nothing to do with 'just sex'. (Perhaps people find this hard to write about because of the words: 'love' is a portfolio of a word, a jingle, a throwaway, a rubber stamp, a lie, a sell, a compromise, a defeat, a defence, a trick, a trash word, a worn word, a pulped and victimised word, a raped, mutilated, bayoneted word, soggy, infirm, a code word, a war word, a dog of a word, don't trust him, unreliable, unbelievable, shot: and 'sex' is worse.) Yet it *was* sex, and it was *love*. Making love, I discovered we could do that. Make love. Out of – two bodies, two minds, vagina, penis, breasts, fingers, orifices several, mouths and tongues, two: one out of two, as they have said. A new one. Made. Spun like silk from a silk worm's innards.

Or it has been written about with pain and a sense of loss. Its absences, its disappointments, its letdowns and failures and compelling inexpressibilities have captured the imagination of some writers. I know that it can be like that. I knew all my life that it could be like that and nothing but that, I thought. But now there's this. When I was younger I read a couple of Henry Miller's books – the *Tropics* – and there was something there. But even then – there was the belittling tone – and it was as much to do with Miller's penis (another unsayable word) and his great horsy performance as anything else. Lots of sadistic, pornographic, ecstatic writhing and rolling, of course. No good that. D. H. Lawrence tried and he could convince – but even he could be very worrying. There is pornography, of course, but that is not the point: the point *is* that it is not the real point.

No. Either it is not possible to describe in detail the intercourse of grand passion or it is possible only in allusions, in hints and metaphors. Direct references bring a snicker and a smirk and to avoid that – to avoid the ultimate horror of being laughed at! – the issue is ducked. Any which way but 'serious'. But what could be more serious and within that seriousness more sensually alive than making love? Inside that 'serious' can be all the pleasures of a life. So be warned, my darling Bernadette, I will try to tell you – how I loved you – no – how we made our life of sex and love (sublime words) and whatever the fusion be called. Separating them has been the problem, I suspect. Love has slithered away unacknowledged by sex; sex has withered unregarded by love; and that third force, the fusion, has eluded description as cunningly as it has so often eluded achievement.

See what an expert you have made me, Bernadette! I do my research, I make my notes. At last I have a talent I can take delight in. I could go back and rewrite that time on the hillside. I could stir in it slowly as I stirred slowly in you; and hover, plunge unexpectedly to detonate a spasm of reaction. I could try all that, but let it wait. Here let it only be recorded that on that night in late May 1989, we made the beast with two backs on a high hillside in the high North of England and it was a wonder of the world.

If I may add two footnotes: I realise that I am missing so much out – there may be a slight chance that you will read this you would be too embarrassed if I described it in detail, as it happened minute by minute. And I can by now take that first evening through almost minute by minute. We walked a little under the moon, holding each other tenderly like caring invalids – and I told you about the old fashion for moon-walking – remember? Your black eyes, black hair, white skin – you stood naked and laughed, kindly, I knew, as I looked incredulously at what was before me – beyond dreams. You held out your arms to form the shape of a cross and slowly turned around. Your white skin lustrous against the darkening hills. It was absurd, it was affected: it can still move me to tears. That image blots up much suffering. We were innocent then. Your skin was whiter than the moon.

You complimented me for being 'fit'. You were specific and emphatic with your praise and I was very pleased. Nobody had paid me such a compliment ever before. I knew I was wiry and all the fell-walking over the years had kept things tuned up. Never have the results of fell-walking been put to such good use! What odd consequences can come from our actions! I went onto the fells to spruce up a life threatened with blight by my marriage and in doing that built up the muscle and stamina which helped me hold and match your young strength.

The other footnote? Another word. Have to write it down. It is a word I avoid although I know that even the best, most praised writers use it, sometimes frequently. I still hate it. I am quite accustomed to seeing it but to say it – no; to write it – no. But it was there that night. So much going on, so many strands I will separate and replait for you but one of them on that thin layer of turf, ancient slate below, was 'fucking'. Why is it that at my age, with the twentieth century hardened to spasm, provocation, crack-up, pollution, turbulence and violent disgust, that the writing of that word – like saying that word in public – should be to me so painful? I feel I have soiled the pages, stained the script. My letter which will not be read, could not be read by you after this because even you, I suspect, might put it down. Or is that merely showing my age and my generation's reverence for the printed word? But I suspect you will find it belittling.

Your brothers and their friends use it frequently and inventively. I myself heard and used it with numb consistency when I did my National Service in the Army. I know that the new younger writers salt and vinegar their prose with it. You must, too, I realise, on second thoughts. It must be the dug-in puritanism of my particular lot. Yet it is a good word. It has a true bite to it, if only I could disinfect the dirty connotation. Does that mean I like and thrill to and want to preserve those dirty connotations? Whatever – the word is right for this first near silent astounding to me bare pelt of hillside love-making, coupling, covering – and what did we say when I was at school? – shagging, screwing, stuffing, riding, poking, *doing*. All shamefaced and disgusting. Perhaps *doing* is the best. And the nicest – there was a fig-leaf of niceness then. Just *doing*. But fucking – (again the shiver of distaste – just as bad even after all the explanation) – we did that too.

And you said, three times, jab, jab, jab, as you went slack-thighed the second time, you said (it was like booms of dynamite), fuck me, fuck me, fuck me!

SEVEN

How could you avoid me for more than a week after that? How *could* you? How dare you? But, Bernadette – how *could* you? Why should I not write this down? I thought you were a cruel, vicious, promiscuous bitch – (your word). 'Tart' was mine. Mind you, in this town, among your lot, 'tart' just means woman. I knew that, so I could use it, you see. Because, although it had a sting it also had a salve. I said that to myself, I would surely bet, one hundred times a day. Maybe a thousand. Damn you! Why did you *do* it? I know I am drunk writing this bit but I read *Booze and the Muse* and lots of writers have been drunks. Maybe they couldn't do without it if that – damn! – means anything. Why did you – even in recollection – OK, I'm drunk – even in memory – why do I not get on the page what is in my head? – for better or worse that is the truth, these are ACCOUNTS! Why did you do it? I hated you. I despised myself. I was a thunderstruck fifty-four-year-old who had 'made love' to you two times on a mountainside and you went off the radar. You drove me crazy and *you must have known you would.*

OK. You didn't say anything. You didn't promise anything. You always had, always have, forever will have a fall-back, a cast-iron, wrought-iron, iron-pillared, any old bloody iron excuse, but damn you, you Border Reiving, Irish Catholic Cumbrian treacherous sexual marauder, I thought. Bernadette!

I love you. Can't you see? Who else will love you like this? Why did you disappear for more than a week? I was in Hell. I know Hell now.

You have shown me many mansions and one of them is Hell. I'll stop. I'll finish the bottle and I'll go to bed. Two and a half paces and fall down. No I won't. It's only 2.10 a.m. I'll walk up

to your house and I'll stand outside your window and I'll howl
like a dog . . .

No. You would banish me for ever.

You banished me then.

And I was on top of a spinning-top of love and sex and mystery
– the whole prodigious universe of life. Now, through you, with
you, I knew that there was a meaning to things. What the
meaning was is a mystery but it was there and we were part of
it and that was life. It made no sense but it was right. After that
night I was hit – you know where? In the gut, Bernadette, in
the gut. I dropped you off and then went home and sat in my
study overcome by this feeling from the GUT, from the pit of
the GUT. It was peace. It was a certainty. It was – it was love,
Bernadette, as glowing, as unmistakable as that bar of electric
heat. It was *me*, beaming out to you. It was the slow heart of
passion, the lovingly cooled intestines of endlessly digested
pleasure, the pump of lust, the corpuscles of anticipation, the
pulse of desire. I gut loved you, gut knew, gut wanted, and you
– gutted me. Ripped me open. Bitch. I didn't mean that – I hate
the word. I didn't mean that. I'm sorry about the word. No good
words.

I will not apologise. I will tell you what I did.

On the first day I reined in my instinct, which was to race to
your house, escort you to work, meet you for lunch, take you
out again after work and head for the hills. I did in fact make my
way down the street at exactly spaced intervals but no luck.
(Curiously, though this merits more than an aside, I felt no guilt
and no fear of being spotted. The lack of guilt testifies to the
total hollowness of my emotional life: the lack of fear, I suspect,
to my profound conviction that I was such a respected member
of the community that even if someone saw it they would not
believe it!) And so I wrote my diary and dreamed of what we
might do.

I made arrangements that evening, I made a revised plan, I
redrew the map of my future. On the second day I knew I would
see you but again you eluded me. Not even the sound of your
laughter and so it was on the third and the fourth day. By then
I was having a seriously bad time of it. Had you been involved

in an accident? Had you run away? Had you been so overcome with remorse that you had taken action against yourself? Images of disaster, each more exaggerated than the last, were projected onto that screen in the skull which flashes warnings and red alerts to the brain. It was then that I rang one of your employers (not Christopher, thank God, his partner) with a question which could not be questioned.

Still nervous, I first asked his advice about house prices, farm prices, land prices, the prospect of growth in one area compared with another: and I gave him some advice in return. Bank managers, even retired bank managers, are a little like doctors: everybody loves a free tip or two. When he was sufficiently relaxed (you see the *care* I took!) I asked him how 'the Kennedy girl' was getting on. I took an interest – the Rotary Prize – something of a scholar – she had asked if she could help me (sorry about the lie) on one of my projects. You were settling in very well, he said. Punctual, cheerful – "That's fifty per cent of it" – and whatever he heard outside the office, he had no complaints, as yet, inside.

What *had* he heard outside the office? I could not stop myself asking that and regretted it. Especially when he trudged into a feeble mess of old prejudice: the Kennedys, the drunken, unreliable, thieving, fighting, strictly a matter for the police Kennedys. But were you there *now*, I wanted to ask? At your desk at this precise moment, 3.48 p.m.? It was too late. He promised to help me sell my house whenever the moment came up, protested busyness, rang off. I was left dangling with frustration at my failure to find out whether you were *there* – I couldn't even achieve *that* – compounded by a protective anger on your behalf that the prejudices against your family should still rub off on you. I went down the street and missed you again. (That simple back door. I did not know it existed. And then, of course, you knew the town like a trout can know the bank of a river: two manoeuvres and you were in the clear.) And so to the weekend and my first taste of humiliation.

Like a lovesick boy on a bike – but in my mid-fifties and in a Volvo, I meandered around the estate on which you lived hoping to catch a glimpse of you. Here I did feel that I was spending some of my credit. Why would the bank manager (retd.) be nosing around this unaccommodating place? No pub (anyway, he doesn't drink, does he?). No shops, so does he have friends down here? Perhaps we could ask if he needs directions . . .

No glimpse of you. No sighting. I never became expert on the layout of the estate. Odd that such a small town as this should so vividly share the characteristics of the great post-war British cities: a virtually scooped out centre; an inner town population largely banished to outlying estates placed at maximum distance from shopping and entertainment; parts of the estates declining towards rubble and taking on menacing properties – boarded-up windows; broken vehicles in front gardens; terminally scuffed paintwork; the unmistakable sign of the sullen debtor. It was down among the debtors that the Kennedys reigned, but I did not know that then and despite my bewildered, parched torment, I was too diffident to ask where you lived.

So where were you? You had gone away for the weekend, with 'the girls'. On a trip to Blackpool. That weekend was the first truly hopeless weekend I can remember. I got through it. Not *knowing* that you were away. Not being able to comprehend your casual callousness. Feeding on that evening on the fells in overwhelming intimate detail. It was then, most probably, that I began to practise the art of recall. I took 'us' through that afternoon – from the terror (and jealousy – only later did I recognise that) of the fair to the highbrowed modesty of the pub to the revelation on the fellside. I found jigsaw puzzle consolation in picking over the details of that, with the discipline of many years still largely intact, with the obligations to Angela and the orderly habits of a lifetime's effort to appear sensible and in control – that got me through. The screams inside the brain became a violent migraine, which was a relief.

On the eleventh day, you turned up on my doorstep, bright-eyed, holding out as a gift a stick of red Blackpool rock.

Before we talk, I have to tell you about something which happened later but which presses to be written down now. It is one of the images of you which I see before me. Both innocent and deeply knowing, unfathomably sexual, and yet it transcends sex. It fascinates me.

It is a pose you held.

In the last weeks I have been in the town library. For the usual reasons: warmth; the daily papers; blotting up time. As a regular I escape most of the pricks of curiosity which can still needle into me as I walk down the street. I have my habitual desk. Mrs Pearson is still disapproving but now she ignores me which is a notch up.

I began to look in books of art and soon became absorbed by the nudes. I compared every one with you and I know that you will not believe this but none is as good as you. Pity there are no painters around here who could – no, don't think that, block that out – you lying or standing naked in front of a painter. Where did I read that Renoir said "I paint with my penis!"? Looking at some of his rather plump and fudged ladies, you can begin to believe it. But the others – Venus, Olympia, the monumental nudes of Géricault, David's perfect figures, Cézanne's solid flesh, Lautrec's diseased flesh, Rubens' too much flesh, Expressionist and Weimar crudities, Judith, the stones and stones of marbled late-Renaissance breast and thigh, how many? – none like you.

And none in this particular position. We had been to bed and were dressing to go out to dinner. You were unaware that I was watching you. That is an essential part of it – your self-absorption and your unawareness of me. There was no audience. What you were doing was entirely functional which is somehow part of its compelling attraction. I don't know why. Perhaps because the absence of an audience meant that it had a different reality from that of all the models and girlfriends and wives and prostitutes who people the canvasses in the galleries of art. You were getting dressed. I realise this is a common theme but *not* in the precise way you were standing.

You were buttoning the suspender from a white garter-belt on to the top of the black stocking on your left leg. You wore nothing else. Both your hands were in play. Your head was inclined, so heartbreakingly reverent, and while the left leg was gracefully bent, the right was comfortably straight, almost propping up the whole body. As your shoulders were a touch twisted to the left (so that you could hook up the stocking) your breasts were a little bunched, presented as it were between

your upper arms, cupped but not in the silly way of eighteenth-century push-up bras or whatever. Everything flowed,
curved like lily petals, the dark hair down over that slender
white shoulder, the breasts unconstrained but shaped, the arms
almost draped down to the thigh, the legs – and such slim-ankled,
lean-calved, long-thighed legs – placed in a classical pose. But
a classical pose is never as unselfconscious and never with the
head bending down quite like that, hair hiding much of the face
like that – the minimal clothes and the contented expression as
if in some silent self-communion, and the bush plain but not the
focus of the scene. You looked up, smiled perhaps, and it was
gone; but it had darted home like an arrow to its target and it
can be and has been recaptured at will.

Why is it so powerful and so tender? Did I as a child see my
mother, or my much older sister, in that pose and did you
reignite a first critical sexual and affectionate stirring? The image
provokes as much longing for affection as for satisfaction. It
seems to me the ultimate erotic innocence. Or is it more damning
evidence of predictable male chauvinism that there is an element
of the naked and helpless victim in this, so preoccupied that she
will not have the chance to defend herself against assault? The
prey? The doe before the tiger. Is it merely that? Or *is* it the
beauty of that line in the pose itself – never seen such relaxed
tension? Or the undress, half-dress, shaping lines of suspender
belt and straps – all those cousins of bondage but also cousins
of form, of the shaping cut in clothes, make-up, dyes, textures,
materials, jewels, feathers, baubles, which enhance and civilise
without obscuring the naked body?

It is an image which I might dare to say 'haunts me'. There,
one evening in an hotel room, as I stood for a moment at the
bathroom door and you simply clipped on a stocking. Two
seconds? No more. And forever.

"I thought you would never want to see me again."

I had taken you away from the house almost immediately –
still bearing your stick of rock – and with tactless importunity
driven very near to the spot where we had made love for so
long, so long ago it then seemed. We sat in the car to avoid the
drizzle. A couple in a car in an unfrequented place – a feature of

lonely suburban road, overgrown lane, remote track, dark alley, underused car park, unlit sidestreet, bare hillside – infidelity and its aftermath in remote stationary cars the length of the land, limbs wrenching against the steering wheel, bucket seats unyielding.

You had taken the initiative.

"Why not?" I asked.

"After what we did. After what I did. I thought you would never want to see me again."

You stared ahead at the drizzled windscreen. I thought of turning on the windscreen-wipers but on consideration preferred the silence and the secrecy. I could not read your expression.

"Why on earth not?"

"You must think me a slut."

"Don't say that. It's not a word that I would ever think of calling you."

"Bitch, then."

"No. Please, Bernadette."

(How I loved saying your name to you in those early days. The three syllables, softly clacking my tongue against my palate. Bern – how urgent, how hot! A – the pause, a sigh the fulcrum of anticipation; dette – the stab, the claim.)

"That would never occur to me either," I added, chiding you prissily – seeking to reassure you, chiding to help.

"So why did I avoid you?" you asked. I was dumb. "Because I was ashamed, whatever you say."

"You had nothing to be ashamed of," I responded quickly, fearing, I admit, that your shame would sacrifice me.

"Do you think that what I did was natural?"

I did. I did. Uniquely, blessedly natural. But I could say nothing.

"You think I just do it with everybody, don't you?"

The thought had not occurred to me. But now it did.

"The thought never occurred to me." It crashed into my mind like water through a breached dam.

"I can't see why not. Especially after the fair."

My mind was whirling, drowning, the fair?

"I thought you were lovely at the fair."

"I behaved like a bitch. I don't know what got into me."

"You were enjoying yourself."

"I was egging you on."

"Why?" This was hope. This was the first irradiation of true hope. You were 'egging me on'. Which meant that you cared for me enough to want to provoke me. Now blaming yourself you flattered me into hope.

"I don't know." You stopped there and were silent. The drizzle thickened on the windowpane. The car had a clammy warmth. I longed to touch you but felt your silence a barrier. Perhaps I had a wild superstition – I did later, on several occasions – a throwback to the black magic spells of childhood, that if I touched you, you would disappear, that would be the end of you, off you would go in a puff of memory leaving me to think – did it really happen at all? Did we really meet and make love at all?

"What do you think?" you asked.

"About what . . . ?"

"You were scared, weren't you? At the fair." You put your hand over mine, without pressure. "I don't blame you. They could've turned nasty. I don't know what got into me. You handled it really well."

"Did I?"

"Yes. You could easily have panicked. Or told me to push off. Or tried to tangle with them. They would've loved that. They would have murdered you then. You just kept your dignity. That was very good."

Your compliment made me blush. You noticed, of course, you who noticed everything, and leaned across to kiss my cheek.

"Fancy being able to blush."

"At my age?"

"Any age. It's gone out of fashion."

Has it? You always could bring me to a halt with a passing remark.

"I'm sorry if you thought I was avoiding you to tease you or be cruel to you," you said, piercing the abscess. "I *was ashamed*, that's all. I couldn't understand why I'd done it."

"Done . . ."

"Let you – make love like that. I had to think it through, why
I let you."

Once more I was sidestepped and left flailing the air. My
throat went dry. You pulled away and sat upright once more and
stared at the multi-speckled windscreen. You were about to
go. I knew it.

"I thought it was marvellous." My words arrived hungry and
whispered.

"Did you?"

"Yes. Nothing like that has ever happened to me before."

That was my declaration. And, miraculously, Bernadette of
the hillside, you understood it and accepted it and leaned over
the awkward space to kiss me on the mouth.

It was the first time for me in the back of a car. It was
agonisingly uncomfortable, undignified, clumsy to a degree,
without grace, brief, unrhythmic, the most cramped, easeful
intercourse which still scorches my dreams.

Were you lying? About being ashamed and thinking ill of yourself
for surrendering to me so fully on that first occasion. If you were
not lying, why did you suddenly decide to turn up on my doorstep
with that stick of red rock? Had you decided I was worth
fleecing? Surely, someone who was ashamed as you say you
were could have written a note (you write so well) or – if so
very ashamed – avoided me for longer, even altogether. But
after a week, when I was stretched to breaking, with the timing
of a torturer, up you bound waving the stick of rock. I thought,
not that night but soon after when Doubts came in like the
Doubts which so savagely assailed my adolescent Christianity,
that a weekend's gossip and laughing about me with 'the girls'
on the trip to Blackpool had been a spur: soak him, see how far
he'll go. You see how early my distrust was sown? Was that
distrust the root of our wrecked love?

How could I distrust you? We drove into the fells and had a
quiet drink and a few sandwiches at a small pub empty but for
us – the drizzle and the sudden sharp coolness – sat close,
looked tenderly at each other, talked about your work. I gave
unnecessary advice and you nodded gratefully. (Was that a
deceit too? Or were the banalities of my experience quite

useful?) You insisted on a discreet route back into the town and would not let me take you home. We fixed the all-important next date.

Angela was unquiet. She disliked the alteration in my routine so much that she had altered her own and come downstairs for the evening. We had supper across the breakfast table and she drank two glasses of sherry which both of us knew would take its revenge. All I wanted was to be alone in my study and write about us which is the next best thing to being together. Angela was perilously overloaded with information from her excessive listening to the radio and she wanted to talk about World Affairs. She was very well informed. Was Communism over – the reforms of Gorbachev being one end, Tiananmen Square another? Did that mean that variations on Capitalism were all the prospect we had . . . ? I made efforts.

When I got to my study I was so tired I could do no more than make a few notes – headlines and jottings which would be enough to evoke the evening and lines of remembered conversation which could be recreated as a dialogue. But I felt so tired. The relief of seeing you left me exhausted. I had not realised how much I had wanted – just to see you – until you were there on the doorstep with the stick of rock. It lay before me on my desk, next to the ruler. 'A Present From Blackpool'.

I slept badly and got up just after dawn. I experienced a great agitation: restlessness veering towards panic. Angela looked wasted. She had been up even earlier to cope with the reper-cussions of the sherry. But her very wasted look moved me.

What was I doing with this girl, I thought? What the hell was I doing? I was not in too deep. I could turn away from it. I could reassert my routine, don my habit. Little harm had been done: we had not been spotted as far as I could tell and if we had there were plausible excuses to hand at this stage. Leave her. Forget her. It would pass . . . All the truisms and proverbs, all the clichés and agony aunts lined up to assure me that it would be no more than a passing fancy, a small failing, a slip, a mistake which could be corrected without too much difficulty. There was yet time. Now was the time. The time to say enough. Common sense's last stand. Not much of one.

I looked up two words in the *Shorter Oxford English Dictionary*: INFATUATION: 'An extravagantly foolish or unreasoning passion'. That was true – though that wicked, loving mouth, the cup of the breasts, the grey speckles in the pupils, made it not so extravagantly foolish. Unreasoning – I accept. But is passion ever reasoning? And OBSESSION: after 'the action of besieging' and 'actuation by the devil or an evil spirit from without' comes the definition for me: 'the action of any influence, notion or "fixed idea" which persistently assails or vexes'. Was my "fixed idea" your hair? Your sex? Your mouth? Your unfathomable switches from rapacity to sweet thoughtfulness? Or was it something less knowable – a floating ideal, rather than an idea, an ideal which fixed itself on what life we could have together?

I wanted to talk to someone about it. To sort it out. Curiously – or is it so curious? – this has turned everything upside down – Angela would have been the best possible person to talk to. But it was too late. It had been too late for a long time now. I was merely philandering with alternative worlds. There was only one now. Yours. 'Actuated by the devil'.

EIGHT

It had all begun too quickly. It was all so messy. Nothing was worked out, there was no shape to it, nothing was clicking through as it ought to have done, plans were worse than useless (worse because the irritation of their failure was galling). There ought to have been a time of circumspection, a time of mutual awareness, a growing warmth, a period of courtship, several serious conversations, a step by step and measured growing acquaintance with the physical side of it. Finally we should have arrived at an adult and thoroughly worked-out appreciation of the situation in which all the pros and cons, the debits and credits, the reds and blacks, the advantages and disadvantages, the plusses and minusses were calculated and double checked. After all, it was the most important matter in my life – why should it receive less close attention than buying some shares? Instead of which we had a hump on a hillside and a contortionist's coupling in the back of a car. Without any *order*!

On paper – and the next morning I raced to paper which soon became my second – but sometimes preferred – way of talking to you – I set out what I saw.

It made very little sense.

(a) A man of fifty-four loses his head to a girl of eighteen.

(b) The girl is attractive by any standards; by some, by his, fearfully beautiful.

(c) He is, at least, reasonably well preserved.

(d) He is married, respected (which matters greatly to him), a happy slave of habit, deep in what he sees as a contented last lap of his life.

(e) She must be the target of half a dozen, a dozen, eligible suitors, lovers.

(f) He makes his overwhelming and incoherent
    feelings incoherently known to her.

(g) She allows him to possess her. Twice.

(h) He suspects she is
    (i) Sorry for him. (But why should she be?)
    (ii) Irredeemably promiscuous. (But this does not
        fit in *at all* with the rest of her character.)
    (iii) In some sort of obscure way in pain for which
        he is a temporary relief. Grateful?
    (iv) Fond of him? (But why?)
        (A) Temporary infatuation
        (B) Longer-term interest

Point (h) (iv) (B) is the key.

I look back on this now and think – pathetic. Even so recently was I that short-trousered prig aching to be a prefect? Order, respectability, controls – all of it the most craven camouflage – against what?

Against you, Bernadette, lying in wait for my life, the ambush I feared and longed for.

I know that people who behave badly often do so from the highest motives. Indeed I would claim to have been one of that self-deluded number. But people can also behave well from the poorest motives. In this town I would say I was thought of as a decent, sound, benevolent chap: all a disguise to glide through the days as if under an anaesthetic. I appeared like that not through any positive or noble qualities in myself but because I was afraid to be other than straitjacketed in convention, automated for civic virtues easy to learn, taking little effort. You exposed that. As soon as I knew what it was I *really* wanted, the habits of a lifetime fled; showing them to be no more than shrouds over the unused furniture of almost six decades.

I spent the rest of the day after the 'Present From Blackpool' in a state of war with time. It continues to be my chief preoccupation outside you. The obvious burden of your longer, my shorter time; the gap of time; the way it roared through us when we were together and underwent so little movement, like an ice-age, when we were apart.

On the day after the red rock I experienced the first of so many days – like today – when time refused to move. I looked at my watch. It was 9.06. I tidied the kitchen, cleared Angela's breakfast, went to my study – forcing myself not to look at my watch, sat down, made more notes, began *these* observations, finally dared a look and it was only 9.28. It was an insomniac's distress. Every minute was ten, every hour six: that day dragged around the prison yard of my mind, time shackled. I was possessed by the thought of you, the taste of your mouth was fresh as rain, I 'saw' you, eyes closed as we made uncomfortable love, my throat was dry with anticipation; finally the feeling became a sensation growing in me like a foreign body which had to be released, had to be exorcised. It was only with the sternest discipline that I could bear to stay in that house and stare out time. I had to wait for our meeting, our date. I did not trust myself to go outdoors because I knew that I had only one route: I was under a spell – your spell – and it was on that day I first experienced it; besotted turbulence. Let this letter to you, let the thoughts I direct at you across the still sleeping town, let the pagan prayers and images of desire work as powerfully on you as you worked on me that day. Because you thought of me, didn't you? You did. You told me so several times and I believed you then: I believe you now even when I have learned to sift through the chaff. You thought of me and finally, iron-clad, resentful, merciless time let me go.

At 5.30 precisely I was waiting for you across the street outside your office. The others looked surprised? Concerned? I don't know. I had no eyes for them. You – took pity? Saw my love? Came across directly and calmly and we went into the pub. What nerve you had! Mine was not nerve: I was numb.

Your territory. You understood that and found the right table. Not in a too discreet corner but away from the pool table and darts board and space-invader machine. Your demeanour was beyond praise – especially in the first hour or two, when I was being as it were 'bedded in'. You played the attentive pupil, I the dignified teacher. Somehow your magic gave me a moat, a cordon sanitaire. You knew that I was helpless, didn't you? You knew that I did not understand what was happening to me – that to stand outside your office so conspicuously was evidence

enough: of helplessness. Your intuition never faltered. In that
moment you – you *looked after me*! I loved that, and you, the
more, even more, for that.

The quiet of the pub and your unembarrassed chatter thawed
me out.

I wanted to ask – where is this going? Do you feel for me
what I feel for you? What does it mean to you to let me make
love to you? Will you make love with me forever? Can I be with
you every remaining moment of my life?

You talked about your job. About the office and Christopher's
pipe. You made fun of the rules and pompous hierarchical
observances. You encouraged me to talk about my hobby. Out
of that came the blissful period in which I outlined the research
trip we (*we* – my first *we* – the deep balm of that), we, you and
I, the two of us, us two, we, together, as a pair, we could take.
It was genuinely based, not fabricated for the occasion, the
seduction. It was as if it were real. And it became real.

You drank vodka and orange; I, halves of bitter which I disliked
intensely but once begun I was somehow stuck with them. To
change would be too much of a statement, break the spell.
Besides – change to what? I was then no drinking man. You
bought two packets of crisps which you announced as 'supper'.
I suspect that very often that was indeed your supper. I lost my
numbness but it was succeeded by an inane drowsiness: a head
unused to alcohol, a heart unshrivelling before the warmth of
you, Bernadette. And you – you were home.

The Kennedys arrived. Not all the four brothers, three sisters, mother and mother's lodger (your father was in the dog-
house at the time), but enough for there to be a parting of the
ways, a tribal presence. It was Friday, one of the two 'big
nights' as I was to learn. You introduced them breezily: "That's
David – he fancies himself as a footballer, our only sportsman;
Theresa – the glamour; Alexander – don't call him Alex, he gets
mad when people do; Joseph – Big Joe they call him, watch that
bloody dog of his, take your leg off" (a pit bull); Noreen – the
nice one; Charlie – her friend . . . The men wore suits, shirts,
open-collared, often folded across the lapels; the women were
gamey, fashionable, I suppose, although I have little idea of that,
cheaply clothed no doubt but, yes, glamorous, not only Theresa.

And loud. Lordly. Tilting back their chairs, eyeing the pool table proprietorially, as it were accepting petitioners who came up for a few moments. This was their kingdom: the clothes proved it. They outdressed the rest. "Old-fashioned," you said, when I somehow managed to intimate that. "Anyway, our mother wouldn't let them go in for jeans." It appears they buy a suit, say for a wedding; it then becomes the 'best suit' (usually of three, two at a pinch) and degenerates in use until it ends up on the building site or the council van, the pipe-laying, the dustcart or at whatever other menial job they do.

That last sentence makes me feel (a) like a snob (b) like an anthropologist. Were these not people I must have seen any day in the town? Yes and no. Passed in the street, heard gossiped about (the fights, the drink, the 'hilarious' family disputes), their weather-pocked faces, mass of hair, ravenous street presence undoubtedly deposited in the inner safes of the mind. But unopened, never to be opened. No bank account; no civic account either.

In truth they were almost as unknown to me as the Papuan tribes visited by television documentary makers. "It appears they buy a new suit/set of head-feathers/painted phallic spear-stick, say for a wedding/moon-feast/war games. This then becomes the 'best suit', the ritualised, initiated, tabooed . . ." We smile but below the surface we are still little more than just such a cluster of tribes in this country: class tribes above all and club tribes, fashion tribes, culture, sport and money tribes, titled tribes, landed tribes, trade tribes, public school tribes and posher public school tribes within tribes who never meet people like the Kennedys who never want to meet them.

I came to see this – or rather to acknowledge it – because of you. You have made me look at so many things afresh and while the results are not original they are newly important to *me*. Perhaps being in love is the nearest someone like me gets to having an imagination. We are still the loose and baggy tribes of the kingdom of Britain and class is our totem and taboo. Ask any bank manager worth his salt!

So your tribe was opaque to me, Bernadette, and alas the more I got to know it the more opaque it became and remains. That night you introduced me. Reasoning intuitively that I was

out of my element, you led me in as gently as a road can lead
you into a painted landscape. Because you did it so casually, I
was casually accepted. Your cunning was litter learnt . . .

I paused then because the flood of that evening submerged
me. Where to begin? This, which began as a letter, has unleashed
so much that I find painful and comforting in uneven measure. I
want to tell our story as well as telling you what I feel, hoping
that it will bring you back. An evening such as the one in the
pub has enough in it to keep me in good cud for days. I can chew
it over often and often and it still holds its taste. So do I write
it for days? Or write *about* the days – days of relief – which are
bearable because of the memory. Or do I let it go and briefly
put it down as a stepping stone to take me that bit further? I
fear to go further. Yet now I realise, or I have decided, that the
end of this writing will be the end of me, of us, one way or
another, I vow, it will be the end. A real ending.

So I want to rush, to meet that ending; and I want to dawdle
because I fear to go further, wanting no ending. And there is so
much I remember. Age is supposed to kill off the memory cells:
alcohol is advertised by A.A. as a brain killer. I age, clawing up
to sixty. I drink, the bottle of whisky a day is admitted. I truly
believe I remember everything about us. It is a bar to writing.
I want to wallow in the recall – I have heard actors on television
say that they can build up the memory like a muscle – perhaps
my concentration on you is achieving that. Yet I want to move
to the end of that sweet evening to tell you what rewards it
brought me.

Avanti! The music was turned down – request of Big Joe
when he saw I was wincing. Inside your family I felt protected
– and a little trapped. Like a lone traveller receiving hospitality
from the inhabitants of a hostile land. Was I being fattened up?
Or were these the laws of the country? David who was 'the
footballer' talked – about football, caring very little that I knew
very little, content to have an audience for his commentaries on
the game. He is charming – a rogue, I soon found out, and I
ought to have guessed this from the way he took me for a fiver
(which you later returned!) and ushered me into a big round at
the crucial time when it was my turn to pay. But I would have
paid five times over. (That was another thing. I must tell you

about it: the complete abandonment of my thrift. Scandalous waste, petty in real terms perhaps, but waste and scandalous and not only did I not care, I *enjoyed* it: it was letting go, it was freedom; it was the new life.)

While we talked I caught phrases from the others and began to piece together what was – still is – for me an exotic life: fishing (poaching), sport (dog racing), gambling (dogs and horses), drinking, occasionally fighting – although that was not mentioned, not boasted of. I discovered to my great relief that I had a reasonably strong head and, by not mixing drinks, by blotting up the beer with sandwiches and crisps, I maintained a pleasurable state of wooziness, a slowed down, mildly soporific, and most benign mood which served very well as the pub filled up and a posse of youths – sometimes young women, even girls, I observed to my astonishment – would now and then race in, commandeer the bar, shout a bit, and race off to another pub, as if hunting for a riot.

The landlady, your mother, you. These are the three I want to write about but my notes on the evening contain less of that than descriptions of the rest of your family. I had never been part of such a group before: indeed I had been part of a group as rarely as I could possibly manage. For that reason alone, National Service was the most testing and disliked period in my life. But I relaxed almost immediately in your group. I was to discover several unsavoury facts about them: this one when drunk beats his wife; Big Joe has seen gaol three times; there is thieving and there has been much violence. So why did I feel so much at ease?

The sentimental answer would be that they were your kin and that was enough for me. Some truth, perhaps. The cynical answer is that they saw me as a soft touch, a useful investment and took care to put on their charms. A sceptical answer might be that they feared that I had discovered how you had spent your Rotary Prize money and were on their best behaviour. (Later you told me there was some truth in that suspicion.) And of course I was a bit of a curiosity – the bank manager – liable, who knew? to turn silly in drink and deliver up one of those incidents of foolishness they most relished. Most of the best stories were of people making fools of themselves or being fooled or, best of all, being made to make fools of themselves. Or it could just have been – as it was – a quiet night. I was not to know at the time that the pubs in the town in which all the Kennedys could drink as a family were down to three, out of the fifteen pubs and clubs. At the others one or more were permanently barred. So this was a valuable asset and they looked after it.

But there was another point. In that gaggle of fine-faced and raw-faced, shifty and utterly confident, inside that *pack*, I felt a tradition – you know how much I loved it – you always accused me of going on about it – a Border history, the remains of and still working out of a unique life which had gone on a few miles north, in the Borders, in the Debatable Lands, for hundreds of years. After the great national fights to a standstill between England and Scotland in the Middle Ages, all this territory had been made into little more than a buffer state, a trouble-free zone, so that the English and the Scots, two aggressive, inventive, warrior peoples, could not easily get at each other again. But in that land – where towns were small and few, quickly destroyed, quickly rebuilt, and the only large settlements were city fortresses or castles or towers, citadels of war – in there had grown families, nomadic, thieving, whose central concern over centuries, over three centuries, was vengeance, whose occupation was war. The Riders, the Reivers, the sheep stealers and plunderers, rapers, looters, the Armstrongs and Grahams, Elliotts, Johnsons, Maxwells, Turnbulls and Nixons and Milburns, the Scotts and the Homes, families capable of putting six hundred men in the saddle, down to eleven-year-old boys, going on raids through the night year in, year out until the two kingdoms united and even then rubbing raw against each other fiercely for three more centuries up until the present. You know how I became intrigued by those families.

Among these were the Kennedys. Sent by the shipload to Ireland (by Elizabeth I), where they continued their vendettas, storming the United States as Scots-Irish, where they were at the unprofitable and dangerous edge of the frontier and took their droving of cattle, their gunslinging, their vengeance with them. I felt that night in that pub that I was in history. Even though, as individuals, they were remote.

Oh, you may laugh, Bernadette. I know your opinion of them all, sometimes your despair. But somehow for me . . . ancient thoughts and usages were still in the air – ideas of honour were still quick and hot and could provoke a bloody confrontation: family name and pride were worn like a proud taunt; the rule of nomadic raiding could still be traced there and the deep notion of being at odds with all terrestrial laws, settling their disputes, obeying their own rules. This was what I wrote about later that night and I like to think that this genuine interest and excitement, the sense of privilege in finding the true descendants of such legendary families sung in ballad, rubbed off on me a little. That might have been why I felt at ease. I was their historian.

As the evening went on I got one or two surprised looks – but nobody stared much – the Kennedys would stare them down: I was in their camp and not to be picked on in any way. Again – that unexpected courtesy, which may be the indulgence of bullies but seemed then to me a leftover of chivalry. But even they could do nothing about the landlady.

She was white-faced, thin blond hair, cigarette never far from a thin mouth, eyes like a spy. Every so often I would feel the force of them and look up to see her sizing me up, quite insolently. She had been there when Bernadette and I came in and maybe in those first few minutes I had betrayed myself. She was beady and unremitting in the intensity of her spying. I felt like data. I was being monitored. The next day – or later that very evening – I would be put through the computer of her knowledge and gossip; and indexed. It was my first whiff of my scandal and I did not like it. In one weak moment I nodded benignly to her. She nodded back, the ash trembling on the cigarette, but her expression softened not a bit. It was I who had softened and both of us knew it. Whether or not a whisper had been in the air beforehand – the talk would begin to circulate around the town now and I thought – please, no; and then I thought – good. Let it be.

Your mother says that she is nine years younger than I am. We established that very early on. She arrived last of the clan with the lodger hangdog and not at all welcomed. She had a word with you, came across, shifted David aside and I was her neighbour and, largely, I remember, her banker (rum and pep) for the rest of the evening. She does not look much like you except for the eyes – the black, the grey glints. And the hair might once have been your colour but it had been streaked and somehow curled – neither operation done with skill but you told me that the 'mussed up' look was 'in'. Your mother is absolutely 'in'. The age of children long past – you the youngest. She puts on the glad rags and hits the town as if all eight of you – *and* a drunken, intermittently violent husband, *and* running battles with the police, local councillors, the rates, the rent, the neighbours and the tradesmen – were no more than an interlude on the way from the front-room mirror to a prime seat in a dangerous pub where drunks rolled in for free and the setting could produce violent action. More than once I saw her light up as one of her boys seemed to seek out a challenge.

She spoke of you – between heaves on a cigarette, large sips of the rum and pep, peremptory orders to the family, loud greetings, shotgun laughs. She spoke of you, but in an accent – local Cumbrian basted onto her original Irish – and amid a din which robbed much of it of sense. The repeated line was that you were 'a good girl' and had been 'brought up with principles'. As time sluiced by, these phrases – and perhaps one other: you being 'a serious girl, no funny business' – became the whole of her speech to me. Music roared, the Kennedys roared, the gangs roared in and out, darts men and pool men roared, and although she was barnacled onto me, Mair (I was given the spelling several times) roared too, pointing her pointed bust like a double-barrelled bazooka, swivelling on the comparatively small waist which cut the champion bust from the once pert little bottom, blood-red-lipped and manicured like a music-hall act, slapping my knee, winking and uttering incomprehensible confidences: I like you, she said, come back home.

As for you. You slid away when your mother came. With relief, I knew that, but I did not resent it because you gave me the privilege of seeing you unseen. You must have known that I was watching you but you ignored it, shut it out. Unselfconscious? I thought so then.

You were at home. You played pool, played it well, played it with the men and did not let their sexual tweakings disturb you at all. When you retaliated it was – as at the fairground – with such a direct hit of language that they fell back, chastened. You taught another girl to play and insisted that she be allowed to learn; 'She has to learn some time.' You were greeted by everyone who came in and greeted them back, always by name, always with an intonation or followed by a question – 'And Andrew, how's he?' – which showed you knew and it mattered, they mattered to you. At one point you were huddled in a corner with a most miserable-looking young man – a boy one could say. Later you told me he had been married for barely a month and had just discovered that his wife was having an affair with a former boyfriend. (Big Joe, who learnt of this, adopted the boy's cause and laid in wait for the unfortunate lover.) You sipped, carefully, I realised, at your vodka and into that combustible, increasingly crowded, unmannerly, shapeless place you brought a pattern, good humour, a love even which hinged the evening. I basked in your skills and triumphs which I thought only I, an outsider, could fully appreciate.

You walked me home and hugged me closely nearby, let me kiss you gently. Failed to tell me you were off on a week's holiday the next day.

But before then, you wrote me the letter.

NINE

What I most admire about your family is their freedom. They have no savings. Banks are to be robbed in cowboy or gangster films. Banks are fat-cat buildings where the rich play games of exits and entrances which mildly intrigue your family. They see a bank manager as rather a comical figure – someone who counts bank notes all day long and is rumoured to steal none of them. I sense that in a way they are sorry for me, to be stuck with such an undignified number or they think I lack guts or guile. There is a surprising lack of envy. That is something else they seem largely free from.

I am not idealising them. I know you said I did when I spoke of the Border Reivers, the historic family quarrels, the deep blood battles which only reinforced by religious and national schisms, that most ancient of struggles, brother often against brother, betrayal, murder, the entire culture nourished on vengeance and obsession with the feud. Perhaps I too easily see the Kennedys as part of that Border history. But on this issue of banks there is evidence. They don't save. They don't defer enjoyment. They don't sublimate. Life is for the living. Money is a means to the constant end of fulfilment. Sufficient to the day. No accounts.

Spending everything becomes the way of life. I saw it that evening in the pub. There was an ease to which I want to apply the word lordly, not to claim aristocratic associations in the English manner which tends to refer all virtues up the social scale, but simply because it correctly describes their owning of the evening, their enjoyment of the historical sports, the talk, the dogs, the tensions. They were on their patch and well content. If the Reaper came that night they could say – we've done everything we wanted, hoarded nothing, lived life as

freely as it was given us – no regrets. Except of course
they would never say anything like that and take me for an
incomprehensible sentimentalist – 'soft' would be their word. I
envied their total gearing to the present. That seems to me to
be a profound freedom. Like so many other clerks of life I have
the past on my back and the future on my mind: regrets and
anxieties, guilts and anticipations, a twenty-four-hour-a-day
shuttle service between the time I will never have again and the
time I may never know. The present is a rare and exhilarating
scent. Your family give it off.

Your letter was part of that.

I did not receive it until the Thursday and you were careful
to tell me that you were coming back on the Friday or Saturday, thus blocking what you might have guessed as my impulse to seek you out on your holiday. You gave no address
which was a further sign – telling me that you wished me to
stay away or indicating that you were so convinced I would
want nothing to do with you that there was no point in filling it
in.

It was bulky in an inadequate envelope and bandaged in
sellotape. By the time I received it I was curdled with bad
feelings. Your tenderness on the night of the pub seemed a
mockery: the memory of the times we had made love seemed
sordid, pleasureless; your sudden absence, yet again, seemed
part of a strategy which I feared to analyse. I walked by your
office four times a day as if the intensity of my longing for you
would somehow conjure your return. Part of me regressed to
primitivism, helplessly believing that wanting, wanting hard
enough, becoming a want, a shout, a cry for you, would bring
you back. You would hear my cry. And I took avoiding action –
to avoid myself – by paying the most careful and loving attentions
to my wife, in taking two particularly exhausting walks on the
far Eastern Fells. Your letter came to my desert not like rain:
it was a monsoon.

You did not know how to begin and settled for 'Dear'. I had
an intuition that you almost wrote 'Mr' and, when I teased away
at this with you later, you admitted as much. Your writing was
on its best behaviour:

I want to tell you about myself. [You began, boldly.]
I want to hold nothing back. I have messed it all up
and you won't want to see me again. But there are a
few things you ought to know. I don't want you to
think too badly of me.

It's raining here in Blackpool and that helps. The
others have gone out with some lads we met last night
and I'm taking the afternoon, the night, as long as it
takes to get this down. It is the most important letter I
have written. I expect it to get no answer. You write.
Just putting it down will help. Maybe this letter is as much
for me as it is for you. But I'll send it. I've promised
myself that.

Well. You met my family and that's how they are.
They were all in a good mood that night but don't be
fooled! Though I say it myself they can be quite nasty.
They turn very quickly. I find this very hard to say
but you have been kind to me. That's one of the things
that's great about you. There's fists fly around where they
shouldn't and most of the women, me included, have
taken several bad hidings. In drink; but no excuse. And
thieving can be funny but it can be bad. Not on any grand
scale, but enough to worry you sick.

What I want you to know is more than this. What I
want you to know – this is harder than I thought. I'm
stopping for a drink.

When I was almost fourteen there was a lodger in his
fifties. My mother's always taken in a lodger or two,
ready cash. This one was a bit different. He had sold up
his farm – the farm had been left to him by his father
who had just died. He was a bit simple and couldn't
cope. He seemed to have no relations – none that he
would talk about. This is very hard. But I have to tell
you. The top and bottom of it was he had money.
"Thousands," my mother said, "tens of thousands."
Probably in your bank! He didn't drink. He didn't much
like my brothers. They were careful with him – not only
because of mother and the money but he was very
big, well built. Liked to sit in front of the electric fire,

watch the telly, go up to the auction on market days,
paddle about on a farm across the way from the estate.

He took a fancy to me. I liked him. He was very gentle
and when he said "Sit on my knee" I did. He used to
give me a pound. When he asked me to kiss him I didn't
want to but my mother got hold of me – when he was out
– and gave me a hammering. It was five pounds I got
for a kiss.

Oh, this is hard. But you have to know.

He started to play about with me. I was well developed
and he would wait until the front room was empty. I
was terrified. He kept giving me money.

One night I tried to tell my mother – and she said I
should count myself lucky because he wanted to marry
me and she had told him that in a year or two I could.
She even said she thought the birth certificate was wrong
– I had been born a year earlier – certainly I looked near
enough sixteen, she said. But I was going to marry
him and we would all be rich.

I suppose I went into some sort of shock. I wanted
to run away but she had thought of that and told the
boys to keep an eye on me. All of them thought it was
a good move, by the way. They had grown fond of
him.

I couldn't bear him to touch me. He had black hair
on his knuckles. Every time he touched me I screamed
inside my head. I *screamed, screamed, screamed*. Black
screams.

The night he raped me the screams came out. He put
his hand over my mouth but I bit his fingers and
screamed. He slapped my face and I screamed more.
Then he started to beat me – about the head – while
splitting me with his violent – sex. The pain from that
as well. I screamed to lift the roof. I didn't know
anything could hurt like that.

My father – not quite blotto – and Joe, suddenly a
caring brother, came into the room – his room – and
set about him. I was banged aside against the wall. David
came in to help and they made a mess of him. When

my mother came in – late – she went for him as well.
The next day she gave me a few slaps but she said that
was to stop me being hysterical. He left the district for
good. They got money out of him. They tried to make
it up to me. My mother said sorry, she was ashamed
even though she had been doing it for my good. She was
frightened. I could tell that.

Somehow I had a hold on them. So when I started to
work hard at school and wanted to stay on after
sixteen, they put up with it. They would never have
done so otherwise.

I've written it. I'm tired now. I want to tell you more
but I'll sleep now. It was horrible, horrible.

I put down the letter at that point and did not know whether I
was going to cry out, or be sick. Darling Bernadette. I wanted
to track down the man and stab him. To pay me the compliment
of confessing all this to me. If I loved you before, I loved you
ten, twenty times more after reading that. To survive that: to
survive it so well. Horrible, horrible, yes. I found I was choking
and checked my pulse – far higher than normal. The trouble was
I got a picture of it in my head – this big lumpen beast and you,
a slender child assaulted. I wanted to drive to Blackpool, to find
you, to wrap you in blankets and nurse you . . .

I read on.

Later.
So there it is. Nothing else is worth telling about my
childhood. Nothing you can't have worked out – just
from living in the town and then meeting my family. I
suppose they are a rough lot – *we* are – and sometimes
I hate that. But then again, with anyone else I generally
end up thinking that things are a bit thin. And they *are*
my own. But I can see the bad side and it is a bad side.
Sometimes I worry because I find that I rather like the
bad side, and take some sort of pride in it. Then I catch
myself worrying and wonder why I do that, why I don't
just get on with it.

I want to tell you one more thing before I write about

us. Maybe it's to put that off. I want to tell you this
because it has a bearing. It was what brought us
together.

At school there was an English teacher, Miss
Atkinson. She was quite young and she could make you
laugh. I suppose she took me under her wing. She got
me to write stories and essays. More importantly, she
pushed books my way. I'd always been a reader but –
after that business – I ate up books. Mostly novels.
Anything I could lose myself in. Anything that took me
over. Miss Atkinson put me onto good literature – and it
would be James Joyce as well as Jane Austen – but I
could and did read anything. Those fat paperback
bestsellers mainly written by women – I didn't jib at
them either. In fact, to be honest, I liked some of
them – they were very outspoken but the details were
good – and useful – and I could get that click in the back
of my head – the click that meant I was lost; for three
or four years that was all I wanted.

Miss Atkinson left six months ago to move to Scotland.
I would have followed her anywhere but she was
getting married. The moment she said she was going I
knew that the schooling was over. University might have
been possible with her backing but even then I doubt it.
There's something about being in our family that makes
it too difficult to leave however much you want to. It
has a pull. Like the town itself. I didn't want them to
feel I thought myself superior. To get on means to get
out and that would put them down. I couldn't do that.
Besides, who cares?

I thought I knew why you were telling me that. It was an appeal.
You wanted me to continue the teaching. I saw us together,
reading in armchairs symmetrically positioned before a log fire;
discussing what I had turned up in the Lakes; visiting castles
and galleries, stately homes, planning trips to the theatre . . .
The idea of helping educate a mind which had achieved so much
after such a wounded beginning moved me. It meant I could be
useful. I could help you. I could give you something worth giving.

"Besides, who cares?" That is how you ended that section and
the question was pointed directly at me. I cared. I care. I will
always care, Bernadette. Let me care.

I'll get round to what I really want to say. I am sorry
if the previous material seems irrelevant. It's just
important to me that you know the main things about
me and as I have no doubt that we shall never meet
again, I had to write them down. We'll never know each
other in the way I dreamed of, so I have some explaining
to do. Basically – why did I do it with you? Why do I
fancy you so much?

You see, it got out that it was you who had insisted I
got that Rotary Prize. I hadn't expected to win it for
a minute. Rotary and the Kennedys! Besides, I was not
going on goodie-goodie to college or university, I was
deserting. But you insisted, they said. So I followed
you.

You never noticed. You don't look round much when
you walk about the town. You are pleasant to people and
you stop to talk to one or two friends but mostly you
get on with going from A to B. Even if you lingered,
I could easily disappear. The place is full of hideaways.

I tried to build up a picture of you, the real you. I
learned about your wife, how she'd been ill for years,
how you are very 'good to her'. Somehow that gave me
hope, didn't put me off. If she was a real invalid there
might be a place for me. I didn't know what place I
wanted or what place there could be. But very soon I
knew that I wanted some place.

What is it when somebody appeals to you very very
strongly? In the books, often as not they put it down to
appearances. I do like the way you look – especially your
eyes and your smile – but it isn't that. I love listening
to you talking but that was later. I could listen for hours,
anything you say, just the patience of it, your own
interest in it. It was something about you. Like a daft
pop song. Something about you. I thought there was

'another' you – whom only I could see – and was just for
me. That's the truth, although I can't explain it.

I wouldn't have dared approach you after the
presentation – when I took more care about my dress
than any time until then. I wasn't going to let you down.
They all expected a gypsy or a slut, didn't they? I saw
the relief in your look. You were determined not to let
them off easily, weren't you? That speech of yours
can still make me squirm when I think of it – but it was
as much *against* them as *for* them, wasn't it? You
rubbed their noses in it. That was great.

Then you asked me to come and see you. At first I
thought you'd found out about the razzle and were
going to haul me over the coals. But I couldn't quite
believe that a hundred per cent. I'd caught you looking
at me at the presentation and you'd switched your glance
away. I went over that again and again – slowing it down
in my mind like an action replay. It was not a cool look.

So I wore stockings. On a summer's night. I knew it
was cheap and in one way I'm sorry. But I'd read those
women in the big-selling paperbacks and believe me
stockings are just the beginning of it! An excuse would be
that I thought it was my first and last chance and I had
to go for it. I calculated. I'd read enough and seen
enough in those magazines on the high shelves, to know
what some men liked. And though I write it was 'cheap' –
I didn't feel cheap. It was exciting dressing to please
you, to meet you. I think that underwear can be a
turn-on, can't it? And perhaps what the women in those
paperbacks and magazines are wearing now is pleasing
because it is the best there's ever been. Anyway, you
noticed. I could tell that you noticed. I fell in love with
you in your study. I felt perfectly happy. I was exactly
where I wanted to be with the man I wanted. Why? I
don't know. So it's out. You were so nice about my doing
research and your helping me. I love that Collingwood
book. But all I wanted was to sit on your knee! All I
wanted was for you to hold me. I knew that you
couldn't – in your own house.

But I was almost certain that you wanted to!

Then I spoiled it. And spoiled it again.

Outside the pub was the start of it. What must you
have thought of me! We'd had too many drinks too
fast and I was well gone. Lucky you were there in one
way to prop me up but I still feel hot and humiliated
about it. I had to cling to you just to stand up straight.
I managed to pull myself together and you were good
enough to ignore it and humour me as we walked some
way together but all I wanted to do was fly. Run away.
Here was the man I respected and thought about day
and night and there was I, tiddly, justifying your worst
fears. That was the beginning of the end. I'd spoiled it.
The most important thing in my life and I'd spoiled it.

That night I went over it in detail. I tried to put the
best light on it. It didn't wash. The more I remembered
– and I seèmed to remember everything, including the
church clock striking and my saying to myself as it
struck – 'Sober up by the time it stops. Sober up!' – the
worse it got. As for the date we made for Carlisle fair,
I thought that you were just being polite. I never
expected you to show.

I thought it would be my last chance. I decided to take
all the risks I guessed were necessary. One of Miss
Atkinson's heroes was James Joyce (by the way, you
are the first and only writer I have ever met, or am ever
likely to: I had never seen a *library* before in a house,
Miss Atkinson had books on shelves but not a library)
and she had given me – as a farewell gift – a new
biography of Nora Barnacle, the woman he married.
Nora was well below him socially, that was one useful
point. More importantly, she seduced him the very
first time they went out together and he stuck with her
forever after. If you turned up at Carlisle I was
determined to do the same. It was a desperate plan but
then I was desperate. I was sick with nerves the night
before. I mean – sick! I had never met anybody like you
and I knew I never would again. But I had to, don't
you see? For that other reason as well. I knew that if I

did it with you I would be cured. I don't care what
anybody says, I *knew* that. I had to do it and I had to do
it with you or I would never be free.

I knew it was wrong and bad. I was long lapsed but
once a Catholic . . . I could not face up to my
conscience about it but there seemed nothing I could
do about it either. Of course there was. Nothing I
wanted to do, that was the truth. What I felt for you,
what I feel, makes me horribly selfish.

I bought that tarty skirt and skimpy knickers. You've
probably forgotten. The one that went up to my waist and
showed off everything including the family silver. I
teased you rotten by going through the fair like a bat
out of hell, as my sisters would. I was desperate to keep
you. I don't know what got into me. The gang who
followed us around could have turned quite nasty and I
was egging them on in a way – to make you jealous? I
suppose so. I think it was something else, though. I was
so excited, much too excited, over-excited, when you
turned up (you had turned up!) and I knew that I had to
go through with my promise to myself and *do* it that
night. I had not let anybody touch me since that other
business. The thought of it sent me into a blind frenzy.
Looking back I did everything I could to make you walk
away from me. Walk? *Run* away!

But you stayed calm. If you had got flustered that
gang would have smelled it and gone for you. And me
I suppose. More shame. I owe you for getting me
through something that could have been very
unpleasant. I was being provocative. I was throwing it
around, to tell the truth, and shame the devil. You just
kept very relaxed. You were terrific. You must have
sensed I was just putting it on.

The talk we had in the pub later was the best time I
have had in my life. It was just like two good friends
talking. It *was* – for that time – two good friends talking.
We had plenty to say without getting nervous about
pauses. Ideas came up and we chatted about them. I'd
read about that sort of conversation and dreamt of it but

never thought I'd have it or enjoy it after Miss Atkinson.
We seemed to go from one subject to another so
easily. You doing most of it, of course. I love listening
to you. You open up. Perhaps because you're shy to
most other people – that was my explanation! Reflected
well on me, see? I could have stayed there forever.
In all – in the little – we did together – it's that village
pub I go back to again and again in my mind. Gentle
and interesting and quiet. That was the best bit. I'll
never forget that. Thank you for that. But it made me
even more ashamed of myself.

   Then I spoiled it all.

   I could not get out of my mind what I thought I had
to do. The only other time I felt that somebody else or
something outside myself was forcing me on was when
I told Miss Atkinson about that business, that rape –
there – the word I hate. I had written a story for her,
for the school magazine, and something about it –
nothing to do with that particular business – made her
start probing. We were in her flat. She lived alone.
She rented a place above the Doctor's surgery and after
he had gone at night it was very quiet. I wasn't used
to such silence. And roomy, a house built for servants.
She had made it very nice with paintings by a friend
of hers, and plants and rugs. I went a few times and
loved to soak up the atmosphere. It was last summer. I
think she led me into it deliberately although I have no
proof of that and certainly wouldn't dream of holding
it against her if I had. Anyway, out it all came – I couldn't
stop myself even though I did not understand why I
was telling my teacher this. Did she want to hear? How
could I blurt out such a humiliating secret? Why was I
doing it? Questions like this were swept aside. I had to
tell her. I was beside myself. I was half screaming and
choking and then we were hugging each other. Both of
us ended up crying. I suppose it is easy to say it was like
confession but it was better than any confession I went
to. I could never have told a priest that. Never. And
I went back other nights to talk because I felt so much

better. And I wanted to show I was better. I wanted
to prove it.

And so with you. I had to do it. I was desperate. To
give you everything I had, all I had. I could tell you
were reluctant. I knew it would break the spell of that
talk. I even knew by then, in some part of me, that
there was no need to grab, no need to bribe you with
sex. But I couldn't stop myself. I should have done. But
I was desperately set on that course.

I had never let anybody touch me since. Even
boyfriends soon moved off because I was thought to
be 'frigid'. It was useful in its way, that tag. I could gad
about and be loud to let off steam without people
rushing to exploit it. There was a boy I did see for two
or three months – but he was just a boy.

There was so much to block out. I remember very
little of that night. I put a lock on a certain part of my
brain, the part that holds the feelings of memory, and
then I nailed it down. I forced myself not to feel. I do
remember calling out the word, the D. H. Lawrence
word, the real word I suppose, the word the paperback
novelists throw around like navvies. It would have
disgusted you, I know. As I must have done, sluttish on
that damp hillside. It worked, yes it worked, didn't it?
But even now I can remember very little detail. I have
tried to dredge it up because it ought to have meant so
much and it did wreck everything, didn't it? But
nothing. I remember later the middle of that night,
though, waking up all but hysterical, wanting to run up to
your house and apologise – even thinking of it as a
possibility until the thought of your wife made me
realise, at last, how selfish I was. I suppose this
explanation is instead of that apology. Yet I have to
say that I was happy and in fact proud to be seduced by
you. You are my ideal. Nobody else on earth could
have done for me what you did. But in encouraging you
to do it, I lost you.

I could not face you after that. And when I did and
you wanted me – again I could not refuse you. I will never

be able to refuse you anything. But it was demeaning
for you in the back of the car like that, wasn't it? Why did
I stack up the odds? It was no good – and yet – I
remember all of it that time, remember how gentle
you were. Even cramped up like that!

But I knew it was all over. Typical that you should
come to tell me – not drop me a note about it. Wait for
me outside the office. You looked so glum about the
whole thing. You didn't have to say it. I knew. I took
you to the pub to stop myself crying in the street. You
could never pluck up the courage to tell me it was all
over, could you? Didn't want to hurt me – that would
have been it. But I knew.

It was strange having to cheer you up so that you
could let me go. Seeing you there, stuck with my family,
bearing with them when you were miles away – it would
never work for you. It couldn't. I saw you looking at
the landlady – both of you knew it was a non-starter,
you and my lot, I mean. I saw it plainly then.

You let me walk back to your house with you which
was kind. You are kind. Perhaps you've been too kind to
me – maybe you should have cut it off from the start.
But you tried to let me down gently.

I'll keep out of your way and I won't embarrass you.
My mother got one or two silly ideas in her head but
when we stop seeing each other she'll soon lose interest.
The same will go for everybody else.

I'm plucking up the nerve to go off and live somewhere
else. It shouldn't be such a big thing to do at my age
but over the last three or four years I seem to have
become welded to this town. Even here, just a couple
of hours south of it, I feel a touch homesick – it's childish,
I know. I feel I must try, though, because I can't quite
trust myself over you – the track record is not too good,
is it? It will be better for me, I think, and a great relief
for you if I go. I must force myself.

So there we are. I find the only thing I want in my
life, the only person I am sure I will ever want to love
and I embarrass you, humiliate myself and mess it up.

But thank you for ending a nightmare. Only you could
have done that. You have no idea how much I love you.
I don't know how to end this, so I'll just say

With love,
Bernadette.

P.S. Don't worry. I won't bother you.

Your intuition was wrong, thank God. I loved you and that
postscript was the final knot. You loved me. I was dizzy on it.
God alone knew why – but you loved me!

TEN

I would call myself a grey man, emotionally a failed man, an empty man who discovered he had one great love in him. If not now, when? If not this, what was there?

I still sweat to think I could have missed you. How many do? How many must. The wrong turning off a street, a non-conversation in a queue, the critical lack of nerve. The lack of daring, lack of courage – only a few are truly bold. Your letter made me bold. Most of us resist the gamble through fear of failure. Near certainty of a rebuff outweighs the chance of acceptance. Most of us manage the effort once and settle with relief for what we get. Or I did. Love turns me into a penny philosopher. We all generalise from our own pennyworth particular experience. Perhaps everyone else out there is bold and daring. Perhaps I am surrounded by couples bound fast in passion. All I know is that I still sweat when I think I could have missed you.

Your letter gave me all I needed. No matter that there had been confusion – life was a muddle, misunderstandings were reassuring, I now think that only simple and straight lines are suspect.

What did enter my mind and lurks there now as a perpetual threat to sleep and peace was the image of you, a slim younger girl, gripped and assaulted by that monster. Alongside the classical image of your graceful sexiness, the clipping on your stockings, this other image squats still and will not be thought away. We had to live, I thought, between the two.

Your letter gave me all the energy I wanted.

But I am evading the main point. I must make sure I don't do that. Make sure I don't assume you know what to me was obvious or understand what most persistently concerned me. Because love can be a cliché does not mean it is any less powerful, or any less tender, above all any less new when someone first catches the infection. Yes it was the first time, and yes I do now think of it as an infection. An infection for which I never wish to find a cure, a disease I am happy to die of. But the way it has overcome my mind and body, the way it has possessed my spirit – soul? it leads you to such reconsider-ations – is more akin to sickness than to health. And yet when the love was active between us, I never felt healthier in my life. Love was life. It drove out all other matters. I rode on the back of it like the boy on the porpoise – free, singing, plunging into the deepest water with joy. But the grip of it, when it is not fed, the way it spreads throughout, charges the smallest nerve ends as emphatically as the heart (pounds, flutters, tenses, shrinks, goes hollow, 'stops') or the mind (panics, fills with rapture, empties, drains, glows, 'bursts') is like a poison. (I guess that all of us first-timers become experts.)

The main point is that your letter was the most moving, gallant, loving, thoughtful, generous, helpful letter I could have imagined. It was a love letter. *The* love letter of my life. The realisation that you were prepared to give me all made it certain. I would have to find a way to persuade you to spend your life with a man three times your age and that man would have to make himself abandon a loved and invalid wife to say nothing of abandoning the conso-lations of respectability. Your letter made me calm.

It also made me so mad with hope that I wanted to race up a mountain like some earnest young actor and proclaim my luck and your name to ever-echoing hills. I resisted that. But that night I instituted what was to prove to be a comforting habit: I worked out the financial equation which could result from a divorce and a remarriage. The variables could be increased at will. The money and property could be divided in several ways depending on degrees of agreement. There was plenty to play with. It was a soothing exercise and at the same time it gave to me the first assurance – the first cheque book – that there could be a future for us.

Us. Your letter was Us. For weeks I could not believe that as I was obsessed with you, so you – not as much I thought, and not as terminally – were infatuated with me. My strategy over the next few weeks was elaborate. It must have struck you either as patient or cautious to a fault. But I had to let the transfiguring news percolate through. *You – loved – me.* I had never anticipated that. I could never have imagined that. But there it was. This incredible gift. This inheritance.

In my foolishness I doubted it even as I accepted it. I could not disbelieve you. Too many years of mummified emotions told me that I could not afford wholly to believe you. In the face of the storm I was, for a short while, cautious, or rather, in a funk.

Do you remember those next two and a half weeks?

Distressing.

I could not keep away from you but I could not pluck up the courage to declare myself fully, i.e. to put my plan to you.

I set out on a course of action which became a pattern and, eventually, a laughing stock. I failed. Remember? Thinking how clever I was, how unobtrusive. Enjoying the seductive thrills of surveillance and completely caught up in my own drama – 'Being In Love'. I was consumed by the fact of 'Being In Love'. And it had been returned. To wake up every morning and know that I was, we were, in love, was to step out of my rehearsal for a life and onto the stage of the real thing. Why did I not sweep you away then and there and give you the talk I had prepared – complete with Debit and Credit, with Long-Term Prospects and Short-Term Losses, a declaration of love as near an annual report as makes no matter? It would have been honest: but I was too overwrought for that.

What I did, in my quiet cunning, was to alert half the town. At the end of those two and a half weeks, the word was out. The bank manager (retd.) was potty about the youngest Kennedy girl.

Did I *want* everybody to know? That is the point, of course. Superficially, I wanted nobody to know. Concealment promised a future. But I was so cack-handed – was I being driven by something deeper? What if, really, I did want 'the world' to know? What if I was determined not to be underhand and deceptive, lacked the brazenness to make an open gesture and yet wanted to signal that we were in love? In that case my clumsy manoeuvring served its purpose. On reflection I am now inclined to think that was the case. I hated the idea of our being less than we should be and secrecy is always less, always, after the first dynamic of dark power, a diminishing factor. I wanted none of it. And also I was proud to be in love with you and loved by you in return: I wanted to strut.

If, in the event, I stumbled that was down to a total lack of experience.

So. I would position myself 'nonchalantly' on the pavement near your office. At 12.25 and 5.25. Five minutes later, you would come out. Then the first scene of the comedy would get under way.

I would look away. I would ignore what I had been waiting for with such a punctual aching heart and look away. More than once when I looked back, you had gone and then began an undignified scramble to find out where you had disappeared. When after further antique mating rituals, my eye caught yours, I would 'express surprise'. Sometimes I rose to 'astonishment'. What a coincidence! Fancy *you* being here! Your friends began by laughing but you must have silenced them because that evaporated and they would shuffle off leaving you alone. Often I could not co-ordinate the legs to direct them over to you. I was truly so clamped with infatuation. Had you not come across on those occasions I would have put down roots through the pavement.

A pattern. At lunch time you refused a drink and refused to go to the cafés on offer – desperate to preserve my reputation but not sufficiently confident to tell me to stop it and stop embarrassing you into the bargain. That, I think, is because you were touched by my awkwardness and also because you did in truth love me and love seeing me. We would end up walking to the church and sitting on one of the benches in the lawned and flowered churchyard, talking about anything and everything. I prevented your eating lunch for two and a half weeks. But the weather was beautiful.

Later in the afternoon there was much the same rigmarole but then we would go into the pub – usually the same one, the one you had sought out the first time, to be closely observed by the landlady who might have been a chemist watching a particularly vulnerable test tube.

Your brothers would come in and to your dismay I would buy them drinks, not observing the most ancient ceremony of 'Yours is the next round'. I paid away merrily justifying it on the unacceptable grounds that as I had more money than them it was somehow OK that I paid way above my whack. Completely wrong, of course. But, practised spongers, they accepted without making me feel awkward. Capable flatterers, they kept me company. I suppose I was buying both their company and the protection – the pub to me was still an alien place, scene of fantasies of tabloid violence.

And I was discovering the puzzling delights of wasting money. All my life I have been thrifty though never miserly. Careful. I had never squandered money. Now I enjoyed doing so. Three whisky and gingers, a rum and pep, two pints of lager and a malt (become my drink – a fortifying habit) and the money was happily flushed away.

It must be connected to what I feel for you. I know that any suggestion of a relationship between love and money will make you taunt me again about my bank manager's view of life, but money began to represent uncalculated enjoyment. It gushed out with an eagerness which insisted it convert itself into life. Love was an unlimited account, endless credit, an interest-free loan for life. And this happened at the same time as I fell so completely in love with you. You are too young to remember a slang word they used to have in the town, one which amused me very much when I arrived here more than thirty years ago: it was 'mint'. It was used for a woman's vagina. It was money.

Darling Bernadette. I said at the beginning of this that my aim was to reconstruct our life together in such detail that it would take up the same time as our affair and see me through. I have made some progress – but those few weeks powder into embarrassment.

All I succeeded in doing was: (a) telling the town I was infatuated with you and doing it in a way which had no dash and no style about it; (b) laying a serpent seedbed of gossip which would spring up armed and oppose both of us; (c) thoughtlessly placing my wife in the firing-line and, although I don't think she learned of it, it was still cowardly to take the chance of exposing her to rumour before I had confronted her with the truth; (d) bemusing you, I'm sure and, I would guess, reducing my stature in your eyes; (e) behaving like a fool – not comfortable to look back on; (f) *such* a fool.

After much thought I have come to the conclusion that I was

unbalanced by your letter. You loved me, you wrote. You
answered every question that my unadmitted suspicions had
raised. More than that, the quality of your love matched mine.
Had I sparked off yours? Had your interest somehow communi-
cated itself to me?

Somehow? Why am I so tentative? In this cell of my own
making, whisky and books are my supporters and I have been
reading works which talk about empathy, second sight, psychic
experiences, extra-sensory perception – subjects which to my
pre-Bernadette mind would have appeared trivial or phoney.
But I know better now. The power of the force called love has
worked on me and I know that if that power exists then there
may well be comparable, allied powers. As I wrote earlier, this
writing is in itself an attempt to get into your mind, sustained
not only by the thought that you might read it but also by the
effect that my solitary concentration could have, across the
town, on your spirit. And so I have brooded on our mutual
obsession and often wondered if it was a spark from you which
ignited me. But even if that is so – what does it say about the
bonfire, the limitless bonfire, waiting to receive the spark? No
– I was alight, and yet:

  nobody had written to me like that;
  nobody had said those forbidden words;
  nobody had loved me like that.

I was as unnerved as a first-blush, puberty-bewildered, fresh-
smitten adolescent. In my sixth decade. Made no difference,
although perhaps it was more painful.

We would snatch an occasional hug in that period – on the
way home. You always insisted on 'setting me back', as you
said, and as you were adamant, I was yielding. (Although I would
often tail you back through the town down to your estate.) And
we would cling to each other, like survivors. I see that I wrote
several times in my notebooks: Survivors.

The serious talk we had was about talks. Rather like matters
of disarmament. We or rather *I* kept saying that we must get
away, on our own, so that we could put things in perspective
and 'talk'. Finally you agreed to that. I had to assure you that

after our final 'talk' I would tell Angela 'everything'. I did not honour that.

I began to dream of helping you become a writer, a lecturer, a voice of consequence; I saw you leaping up like a young salmon and conquering the steps of a fall so deeply and historically organised against you and your kind. I wanted to coach and coax you up the river to where the clear sweet pools of life were.

We did not make love at that time. Although I shivered with longing in your arms my restraint was total. You felt my need. Later you told me that it was the 'best thing' I could have done, that writing the letter had brought back all the horror of the rape, that what you needed was uncomplicated comfort. A hug. So at least that decision worked, although looking back, perhaps it was the fact that we did not make love which made me, at least, behave so very clumsily. The consummation of love, I found, gives you grace. Take it away and, as usual, you stumble.

So out of that exposed embarrassing time came some good, came that healing time.

And then we went away.

I hoarded my respectability. I now realise that I have lost it. Once I knew its value. The up-to-date writers I read – or read about in my quality daily and my quality Sundays – seem to give not a fig for it. There is no norm, it seems, and no outrage. Respectability is foreign or unfashionable – I cannot fathom which.

Well, speak as you find. In this town – and perhaps elsewhere (even London) – respectability is not dead. It may have changed its appearance a little. It may be under the surface of tolerant conversation and seem to yield very low interest. It may be retreating somewhat (or is it regrouping?) but it persists. I have been part of it and it works. You may say I invested in it and others invested in it through me. This town knows respectability, certainly my class and generation and, scrape a little, a good number of yours.

I wrote that 'it works'. I mean it can make life better. If you learn the rules and accept them and enjoy them, there are considerable benefits in order, in social tranquillity and in a shared sense of being the good ones. Priggish? Certainly. Dull? Very likely. Oppressive and deadly and hypocritical? For some.

For others, a well-signposted, soundly surfaced way of life.

It works because it takes care of so many things. The ultimate respectability is the deeply ordered, minutely organised life of a nun. All respectability tends to a religious order. There has to be something which inspires faith. Our small-town faith still lay in civic and social acts of the professional and business class despite being blasted by statisticians and torpedoed by shock revelations in the press: monogamy, financial probity, care of family, public politeness, public sobriety, a general interest in the welfare of other members of the respectable class, involvement in respectable activities – Rotary, the Inner Wheel, the Bowling Club, the Church, various committees. Of course there were 'respectables' who broke these rules. But they had to be regarded as the exceptions, or even as tolerated eccentrics. It could be reduced to one commandment: never disrupt the public discipline of a polite club.

Once this useful formula was followed, you could, I discovered, be surprisingly free. Not as free as the wind like the Kennedys – and *you*, you above all! – seem to be. Not gypsy free, footloose and fecklessly free. But for a man in my position surprisingly liberated. You need make no close bondings of the sort which can drag you down. You need give very little away, very little of yourself. You could be completely selfish and feel good about it.

True respectability is the perfect seedbed for a secret life, a double life. Your brothers do not need it and would not endure it. I needed it and came to enjoy it. The double-ness – my true, private non-involvement with all I seemed most attached to – gave me a great *frisson*. I was in counter-intelligence. I was a spy on myself. I could enjoy the undoubted advantages, the ease of this respectability and enjoy equally mocking it by what I saw as my quite other life – being a Lakeland writer!

When it dawned on me that my respectability had gone I was like a knight suddenly without his armour. You would have thought that I was wholly prepared for a double life with you. Yet without the feeling that I could rely on respectability I was lost. Respectability held me in a firmer vice, controlled more of me than I had imagined. Respectability worked until it met – you, Bernadette.

ELEVEN

In retrospect, failure can be entertaining. At its best it can be helpful. At the time it is a dog. Our first – escapade? Adventure? We even failed to find a word for it – was the sort of failure that gives the word its bad name. I ought to be able to look back on it with amusement or nostalgia but I can only wince at the clumsiness of it all and regret that time – the old enemy – was wasted through my stupidity.

How could I fail to confirm the hotel rooms? I, who had worn braces and belts in every transaction of my professional life. I, who had never knowingly left a list of figures un-rechecked. I thought a call was enough and believed the merry young voice at the other end of the telephone when she told me "That will be fine, sir. We'll expect you at six."

But this was the Lake District. It was a busy time of year. Moreover, the hotel I had so astutely chosen for its moderation in all things was precisely the quality of place most sought after by those in search of hard walking and high thinking. As you know, we arrived at 7.30 (I don't blame you – my arrangements were too complicated) and we were turned away.

I remember standing in that rather smart reception area – confounded. My brain refused to compute. The girl (the owner of the merry young voice?) took pity and phoned up neighbouring hotels until she came up with one.

They only had a double room. I had booked two singles. I repeat all this to you because of the moment which then occurred – a brief moment in real time, but a stain on my memory still. None of us knew where to look. The girl, I *know*, suddenly divined much of the "awful truth": you refused to let me catch your eye. So it was left to me. I could not respond. Patiently, her hand cupped around the telephone's speaking piece as if she were concealing a cough, the girl waited.

It *had* to be two single rooms! Your letter had affected me deeply. I thought that I might never be able to make love to you again and I wanted to *prove* to you that IT DID NOT MATTER. You had praised me for being considerate. Nowhere else? I asked. Not at this time of night. (7.40!) Only the double room.

I felt that I was taking unfair advantage, that I had knowingly tricked you – mad as that was. That this was ruin; above all that I was incompetent. "We expected you to confirm in writing, sir."

For how long did we stand there?

In part I stand there still. The old fool, the young girl, the patient receptionist.

At last, you said, *sotto voce*, "We'll take it."

And then? Humiliation yes, but the unsettling sap of excitement. We would be sharing a room! We would be sharing a bed!

A room? We had to flatten ourselves against the wall to move in it.

A bed? Two army issue single boards rammed together but made up separately so that they were still, in effect, single beds. Bound apart.

While you dressed to go out to the pub – it was a boarding-house, we were too late for the evening meal – I retreated into the cupboard of a bathroom and stared at myself in the mirror until my face became unfamiliar and I repeated my litany. I was a grey man. I was an empty man. I was a continually failed man with perhaps one, this one last chance for love in me. I knew it did not matter a bit in the great scheme of things – but it mattered to me as much as life itself. It was life itself. The only force of comparable value was time and its inevitable conclusion. The exaggerated declaration of poets learnt at school, the inflated declaration of popular songs – both now struck me as being just about right. Except they did not quite meet the case. They had not met you. I stared at myself as if I were staring at a stone and for a moment or two I thought I ceased to be a creature and became a thing. Somehow it helped.

And you were dressing. Your hair would fall over your eyes. The beauty spots, then uncounted, troubling you. A wriggle into the white tight skirt, flaming-red belt, red shoes, black satin blouse and then the merest dab at your face. "OK," you sang out and I emerged to see you in town splendour in that pinched room. My cravat and corduroys seemed a little rustic, with the brogues, especially as the sun was still holding its northern long-day heat as we walked down to the pub.

That short saunter gave me some moments of equilibrium. I could have been your father, I said to myself and to the host of mockers and accusers who danced around the outer circles of my brain; we could be teacher and pupil; or just good friends as they used to say in the newspapers. It is possible to be just good friends. At that time it was the most I could hope for.

A glorious evening. The mountains full circle around us, protectively. The small lake glittering and needled with the long sun-rays. Despite the unusual early summer heat, the full complement of greens, the colour of life, here superabundant and luxurious in variety and texture. A blue darkening sky unblemished by any cloud. That unique sense of space, cosiness and splendour. You put your arm in mine. Our first night away would work! Even the beds seemed a blessing: twinned but separated, joined but single. And I was in what had become my element. I remember showing it off to you, naming the peaks, mentioning the poets and painters (surprising myself with what I had accumulated over the years) as if the Lake District were somehow my own grounds. The more I chattered the tighter your arm tugged mine and, Bernadette, on that short summer walk, which I can retrace as I sit here in the midst of winter, even, when I concentrate, call up the precise pressure of your arm on mine, I would not have changed places with any man. We were home.

The pub wrecked it. Or was it me? Was it my stupidity in telling you "It didn't matter" when you were so obviously right? "I can't go in there dressed like this," you said, the instant I opened the door. The weather had stayed some drinkers out of doors and I ought to have had the common sense to stay outside. But at a quick scan I could not see a table. (Why did I not make for the wall? Was it because of the half-dozen young men already strewn beside it, eyes, as I thought, already casting looks at you?) So I ushered you inside.

In winter that pub is a nest of pubby virtues. In spring it is delightful, in autumn with the first log fires, the drawn curtains, the new prominence of the seventeenth-century beams, the horse-brasses, the decent dark wood furniture, it is at its best. In summer, with the tide of tourists unpredictable, you have to be lucky. Lucky for some was what we saw – a cauldron of young people, booted and swarthy from the heat and the exercise, amiable but loud. Like a company below decks on a gunship after a battle, all fired with stories of the adventures of the day – the rocks, the screes, striding across the tops. You came in like a hummingbird to a rookery. Not that you were apprehensive or in any way timid. You could have booted them out! "You should have told me," you whispered. "Told you what?" You ssshhhd as I spoke – for I raised my voice to beat the din – and for some time I could not understand your agitation. We went to the bar – the young people were quite obliging and made a space for us – but once again I could see nowhere to sit. You ordered a half of bitter which was unusual. Behind you, some of the girls – in baggy shirts and jeans and climbing boots – were drinking pints.

I ordered some pub food despite the fact that you said you were not at all hungry. I thought you were being polite or shy; or perhaps I only half-heard you – the noise was not something you could get used to and the roar of it was a grim obstacle to conversation. I could have wished for a quiet corner table, a chance to plan the next day and decide on which route we would take but that was impossible. It was difficult enough to hold your drink steadily as the friendly jostling and nudging scrummed around the bar. I thought you looked quite wonderful. Easily the most attractive woman there. Certainly the best dressed.

But there was the problem. As you told me quite patiently later that night. Too well dressed. Wrongly dressed. Out of place and therefore feeling ignorant and because of what you called the 'unisex fell boot look' which ruled the fashion, rather vulgar. "I felt out of it, so I wanted to get out of it."

I insisted you made some inroads on the prawn salad. I was sure you had not eaten all day. Of course I appreciate the difficulties you were having – it is not very easy to keep anything on the plate in such circumstances – but when I smiled (conversation was impossible once the music – a guitarist and a harpsichordist – began) you smiled back. And they were an amiable crowd. You had eaten what you wanted far ahead of me and I was left with rather a lot of Cumberland sausage, bacon, onions, a coleslaw salad and a precariously generous helping of chips. When in dumb show I indicated that I would like to eat a little more you nodded encouragingly and indeed the music seemed to cheer you up. You turned to face the guitarist and began tapping your feet.

The guitarist stared right at you, and grinned (leered might be nearer the mark, I can see him now), revealing an overlarge cluster of overwhite teeth. He nodded away as if he were serenading you. Courteous as ever, you smiled back. I know you did it as an act of good manners, as the automatic, unthinking response of a warm nature. The effect on me was physical.

I was about to write 'It was as if I had a spasm, a constriction which affected my throat and my stomach, a cramp.' But it was not 'As if', it *was*. Jealousy struck like a clash of cymbals on my ears. It was dizzying, brought on nausea, left me bereft of energy and yet filled with this terrible uproar. In that blitz I suddenly saw your anxiety for what it was. Of course I should have told you that this was a walkers' and climbers' pub; of course you felt out of it in your town clothes; of course it was no fun to be barged about by big-limbed red-faced youths while standing hunched over a rather badly served prawn salad! We had to leave.

But you did not want to leave. By then you had shrugged your way through the singularity of your position, dismissed anyone (was there anyone?) who gave you a pitying look and decided to make the best of it. Or was it more simple than that? The guitarist was a handsome chap; he was talented. He was younger than I was.

It became an unbearable duet, he playing to you, you applauding him, rewarding him with your eyes, your smiles. Keen handclapping marked you off from the desultory reaction of a crowd which would have been just as happy left to its own company. As I would. When I suggested we leave you said "I'm just beginning to enjoy it" and, mischievously? "You haven't finished your sausage." I could not eat. Halfway through his next piece I excused myself and went out of doors. The young gang there seemed to turn and mock me – how self-absorbed one becomes! – and I walked some way down the road to take in deep breaths. For a moment I thought that I would be violently sick. That was succeeded by some minutes of trying to prevent myself shouting out loud – in order, I assume, to let out the pressure of jealousy.

It is a demeaning, an unattractive and useless emotion and I was ashamed of myself. It was also new. As new – and really, now that I think back on it and so easily summon it up – very like the direct hit of love I felt for you. I understood, immediately, that it was a destroyer. There was every reason why he should smile at you – after all, you were not only the most attractive person in that burly bar, you were the most appreciative of what he was doing. As for you – you were, you are, free to like whom you choose. You have a naturally quick and open response to people. What more natural? And the age, of course. I never ceased to fear that gap of years between us. Not then, not now.

Wild thoughts scudded through my mind. It was as if that resplendently calm evening had suddenly become a storm-infected heath: that I should leave you, that you would leave me, that I was utterly foolish, that you were being kind to me, no more than that – images of you away with the guitarist, of me racked with sorrow (self-pity arrived with love and jealousy) – a piratical crew of emotions boarded me and took me captive. Suddenly pricked by the simple thought that I was giving the guitarist a clear field, I rushed back to the pub.

You were sitting on a bar-stool, your lolling red shoes somehow the brilliant focus of the room, your hair all but obscuring your face as you bent over the guitar. He was standing beside you, his fingers over yours on the neck of the instrument, encouraging you to strum away. A not inconsiderable crowd was enjoying the lesson. No, enjoying the chance to look at you. And when you looked up – and saw me – your face was divine. Such happiness and peace! Such pleasure – such innocence? I had to believe that, even though the green monster was thrashing about in my intestines, its tentacles tearing faith and affection from me. The heat choked me. Only love could throw it off, could salt me free of it. I knew that. (My education in instinct was being given another thrust.) I forced myself to smile. I forced myself to walk towards you, casually. It was very difficult.

"This is Ray," you said. "He used to teach me when I was at the Junior School."

Ray shook hands. Ray had moved away from the town about ten years ago which meant that another alarm bell could be switched off. Best of all, Ray was married and his wife was about to join him in the pub and she was most welcome. I bought the drinks to celebrate and to drown my unworthy suspicions. Ray and I shook hands once again when we parted. Ray was a great man.

We sauntered back. We ought to have been reconciled. But on that brief walk – perhaps your embarrassment returned, certainly my jealousy did; more than likely the prospect of sharing that small room unnerved me. You too? The mood of surprising joy which had floated us down to the pub had drained away.

Let me hurry past those awkward minutes when we attempted not to see each other undress, wash, and go to bed. Afraid, it seemed, to look at each other: disturbed at the prospect of making a noise while on the lavatory; wanting to define separate spaces in a space too small; who would use the bathroom first?

In bed you turned and kissed me, as I thought, briskly: as if you had been administering the goodnight peck for years. I lay there, flat on my back, fearful that if I slept I might snore; it was you who, lightly, sweetly, snored.

And where was the desire for you? We were in beds, side by side – a bed each. You had given me no spoken indication that you would resist if I were to make advances to you. But I stayed in my own bed, even though, as your sleep deepened and my wakefulness began the long night's journey into discomfort and frustration, I started to want you and grow to want you most powerfully. It was the image of that lodger, the man you had written to me about. I wanted to talk to you about him but I could not. Writing was one thing; speaking it face to face proved a far more difficult ordeal and it was a couple of months, I think, before you were able to talk about him. He was between us.

He made me feel unclean. He made me ashamed of our previous couplings, ashamed of the way men assaulted women in love-making. Yet I wanted you. It was a night when time played some of his meaner tricks, freezing the hours, inflating the minutes, sometimes refusing to budge. While my mind grabbed at the speed world of fulfilment and hope, my body lay numbed in a time stupor on that board-hard bed. Between the lightning of fantasy and the slow stop-progress of aches and pain, our first night together steered its exhausting chaste course.

In the morning you turned to me sore-eyed. Why had you been crying? "Because you didn't want to make love to me," you said. "And," you added before I could begin to present my case, "you thought I was flirting with Ray. You were jealous, weren't you?" The wind was out of my sails. "What do you think I am?" I was transfixed by your beauty. The light came strongly through the thin curtains and your white skin yielded to it; your breasts rose above the sheets as you turned to accuse me. "Why did you not come to my bit of the bed?" The confusion of answers was too much for me. I began to stutter out explanations where I ought to have said nothing, and reached over for you, and held you. But it was the time of explanations and out they came, each lamer than the last until they limped away in hopeless retreat. You got out of bed, stood, back to me, and stretched widely, fingers pushing every millimetre of you to your fullest extent. Why did I not reach forward, encircle your waist and bring you down to the bed?

It was the image from your letter. I did not want my actions to follow, to mimic, his violence. When I told you that, some time later, you understood.

We were very tense. The gong sounded for breakfast. It was a call neither of us wanted to answer. We agreed to find a place for coffee somewhere along the road. Again the awkward charade. How many times did we apologise to each other as we bumped across that tiny room. 'Sorry.' 'Sorry' became the only word we spoke to each other.

I had failed. It seemed too late to hold you. Too late to start. This night together so anticipated, so discussed, so daring in its way, had dribbled away into a very English nothing.

You pulled on new trainers – red and blue – and caught me

looking at them from the majestic composure of my over-dubbined boots. "I suppose these are bloody useless as well," you said and burst into tears and threw one of them at the wall.

Then, then, then and only at last then, I took you in my arms. You clung to me as if drowning. You shook with crying, all the time trying to stop and criticising yourself for being so 'stupid', so 'weak', so 'soft'. But you cried for minutes on end and as the tears left you so the tension left you and so it left me and finally we undressed.

It was then that I counted the beauty spots. Then that we made love so gently it passed belief. Two hours later a firm knock on the door reminded us that "Checking out time is eleven and it's ten to already". I uttered a cheerful sound in response and we played the game. Got up. Looked not without pride on the wreckage of sheets, the disarray of pillows.

After that I did a sensible thing. I took you into Keswick and equipped you top to toe. Anorak, pullover, cords, waterproofs, thick socks, rucksack, compass and finally the very best brown leather climbing boots. And a tin of dubbin. You wore the lot and we went back to that pub for a bar lunch. You ordered the sausages.

"I want to marry you."
    "You can't."
    "Why not?"
    "You're married already."
    "I can change that."
    Usually you were silent at that point or you said:
    "I don't want to talk about it."
    "Why not?"
    You would shrug and stare into the view or if we were in bed you would look away.
    "You don't want to be hitched to an old man."
    "Don't be silly."
    "I don't blame you."
    "Don't be *silly*."
    "Three times your age."
    "That isn't the point."
    "What is?"

Again you would be silent. Perhaps you would trace a route across my skin with your index finger. Or tug me very quietly towards you and give me a kiss.

"Why don't you like me to talk about it?"

You would shrug.

"Does the idea disgust you?"

"Please!"

"It does, doesn't it?"

"There are better things to talk about. I love to hear you talking. This just spoils it."

"What do you want me to talk about?"

"Anything."

You meant it. You made my talk live. I told you things which surprised myself, incidents I would have sworn dead to the memory, stories of my childhood, the first years in the town and what I thought of it, the bank, the Lakes. Anything to do with the town delighted you: to you as to the older generation, its goings-on were a soap opera and a chronicle. The Kennedys are old-fashioned in that as in so many other matters. You made me want to tell you things. Not that you laughed at every opportunity – I still think that some of my drier remarks passed you by! – nor are you any inch a flatterer – but it was such a pleasure to talk to you. I suppose that is what actors and actresses mean when they describe a 'good audience'. You were my audience and because of that I discovered that I wanted to talk.

Now and then I would hear myself sound like Professor Higgins in *Pygmalion*, but you lapped it up. You must have been a joy to teach. I found that over the years I had accumulated a tidy pile of information about the district. It was like popping fish to a young seal.

Was it my fancy or did you bloom? Your face grew less prone to that defensive set of the jaw: your eyes began to lose their hurt, even rather glowering expression. You adapted yourself to the habits of the new places – the hotels and country pubs – with swift ease as if you were relieved to be adopting a different character.

"You ought to go to university."

"Do you want to be rid of me?"

Oh no! No. And the fear that rushed in stopped me dead. University – others her age, bright young people, many from backgrounds she would find glamorous as they would find hers exotic . . . A tight muscle seized my throat but I had to speak.

"I would pay for you."

"Would you come along as well?"

"Would you want me to?"

"No. Rather go on my own. Get in with all that young student crowd!" You teased me like that sometimes but instantly, recognising that I was pathetically downcast, you picked me up. "Don't be silly. I'd rather be with you any day. Bet they're all snobs. Anyway, who would want to leave here?"

You were becoming as fond of the Lakes as I was. It had been a foreign land to you. The outer Northern Fells were only a few miles south of the town, but the Kennedys were no tourists.

"I feel at home here now," you said. Perhaps seeing the hills every day had raised your mind ready for walking them and discovering what had gone before.

I would look at you. So beautiful, hair luxuriant, face fresh from the fine weather, always a smile puckering the corner of your lips, eagerly scaling up some rocks, stripping off that day at Ellswater when the heat was oppressive and wading into the gunmetal water, suddenly dropping asleep like a bird on a branch as I drove back towards the hotel, your head nesting on my shoulder, the smell of the heather in your hair. I had to struggle not to look at you all the time and drive us off the road.

Tchaikovsky, Sibelius and Dvorak on the cassette – humming the tunes, letting the romance stir the senses. They sounded like we felt – both of us said that. And Elvis, the Beatles, Bob Dylan (I had admitted my liking for none of these to my staff) singing along; my youth. You knew the words better than I did. The car went with the rhythm, the countryside went with the music, it made us free; there was a spell on us and it was as if we hovered over the place, sailing on air bubbles, swooping at will, wingtips touching; one.

You were a wonder to me. That you were you. That you loved me.

"Really?"

"I think so . . . Yes." Spoken quite solemnly, even matter of fact.

"I can't believe it."

"Why not?"

"You're so . . ."

"Not that again!"

"Lovely! And so many men must –"

"None like you. I don't know where you came from but none like you."

"Is it because I love you so much that you feel obliged?"

"Could be . . . Oh God! *Teasing*. Of course not. You can't be obliged to feel what I feel."

"And what's that?"

"Come here and I'll show you."

"Show me what . . . ?"

"Show you this, and this, and this."

It was seeing you grow. How easily you learnt what to do; how fast you digested knowledge and were able to use it to make a comment; it was like being with a brilliant student. It *was* being with a brilliant student.

And you were so pleasant. To everyone. The waiters and waitresses, people we met in the pubs, your good nature embraced them all so effortlessly. I watched in awe as you made so light and yet so much of those glancing relationships which to me were so stiff and so meaningless. I discovered that the woman I loved was also lovable. It would have made no difference, I guess, if you had not been. There is nothing I can do about loving you – couldn't stop it if I wanted to, couldn't stop it if I tried. It is as if you have merged into me as you see happen on the screen with trick photography.

Of course I saw myself when young in you. Except that you seemed so well balanced. I thought a good deal about that. Was it that terrible incident which had crushed experience into you? Or was it the freewheeling, uncontemporary ways of your family-clan which gave you such a poised view of the world? Certainly very soon I felt an equal companionship which owed more to your maturity than my attempting to become young again. I wished myself years younger: you took no notice and often enough that disarmed me.

We enjoyed so many of the same pleasures. At dinner, commenting – in whispers or in code – on others. How soon you became used to the small elaborations of dining out and how quickly you enjoyed it – as if you had been weaned in restaurants on good wines, nurtured by service. We guessed at occupations, relationships, and tried to guess at the conversations of others.

You were a delight. I had never known what it was like to be with a delight, with someone I wanted so much to be with and who wanted so much to be with me. But I could never stop the questioning.

"Do you think this could go on?"

"*You* go on."

"No. But is this just because it's new or could it last?"

"Doubt it."

"Bernadette!"

"Do you have to be serious?"

"Could it?"

"I think it could."

"Will you marry me?"

"Can't."

"I'm married already?"

"Yes."

"And if I say I'll look for a divorce?"

"I don't like that word."

"But would you marry me?"

You never said yes but nor did you say no.

"Why don't we just stay as we are?" you said. "Why do you have to force it?"

Was I forcing it because of my age? Very likely. And yet, as I remember, I felt more balanced about the subject at that time. Oh, I know I nagged on about it – but that was partly as a joke, partly, I suppose, seeking reassurance and partly to flaunt it, and exorcise it.

Fifty-four is no great age today. When I was young, fifty seemed the last watering-hole before senility. Now people go up Everest at fifty; they run marathons at sixty; they cycle across France at seventy; at eighty they found a new dynasty and the ninety-year-olds take up ballroom dancing. I have led a moderate life: a non-smoker – there was a pipe in the early days but it grew too tiresome and after the pipe cigarettes were tame; until recently a very occasional drinker. Inadvertently over the past years I have taken a lot of good exercise, nature's way, pounding up and down the fells, the full blast of fresh air. My mind is active – that is supposed to help according to surveys I have read. So, fifty-four and fit. I did not feel foolish as in the very early times.

There have been odder matches, I'm sure. Not only in times past when the custom was for older men to pluck the budding girl, but often enough today when a first wife dies and the second chance uses the opportunity to begin again. So in twenty years' time I will be seventy-four and you will be thirty-eight. (a) We could have had twenty good years. (b) There are Prime Ministers and Presidents and International Business Entrepreneurs and working Artists who are seventy-four – why should being a husband be so much tougher? (c) The point of your letter – which I still find it hard to believe – is that you liked me – and that must include the fact that I am so much older. It could well be *because* I am so much older. (d) If I drop dead you still have time to marry again and have a second go. With a good inheritance.

I have to shake off my own prejudice about age. The world where older and old people are to be seen but not heard, dumped in the nursery, looked after by the servants of society and only brought into adult company for short periods and on their best behaviour is a world I reject. You live flat out until you die. And until you die, all things are possible, all things are to be attempted, nothing is to be given up just 'because of age'.

I felt uniquely, urgently, extraordinarily well in those weeks as if my body had reactivated its blood and chemicals. And there was a much deeper upheaval. It sounds too much – or am I still, even now, stuck in my blind, enclosed past? – but in those weeks and months I, we, felt part of an intimate time or space, to do with the stars and oceans and with music . . . We had that. Life was boundless. And I was bursting with the torture of being with you. The rest of the world could never be as happy as I was with the woman I would marry and love for ever.

TWELVE

Over the next two or three months a life was lived up; never was I so alive. I never knew there could be such joy. An old word from the hymns and psalms of churchgoing days. But *the* one. *Joy! Jubilation!* You loved me then, I am sure, at least some of the time and intensely some of that time. I worshipped you. And I discovered, I suspect to your great surprise, that – this is to quote you – "I was very good. Really very very *very* good," you said. (At sex.) It took an effort to write that but it is a true part of our story and I must not run away from it.

You said that you had never known what 'making love' meant; you said that you did not believe what you were experiencing – we together 'made' this invisible link. You said words which made me so confident and insatiable that our love-making could go on for more than an hour – you know that I do not exaggerate – stop, because of satisfaction – often for both of us – and then, quite soon, begin again, this time for longer. And then yet again for hours – the best of all – a time for experiments and conversations in coitus, until erotic exhaustion set in and we fell asleep, dreaming of what we had just done, the dream merely a continuation; and we woke up to the same reality. It was a miracle, Bernadette.

This document is for you and so why do I tell you what you already know? In case you have forgotten. In case you wish to forget. In case, sadly, you never did know. You cannot know how much I love you – or is that arrogance? Do you in fact know and has that knowledge scared you off? That is a possibility. Love can be suffocating. It can be intolerable to be overwhelmingly loved. The unregulated passion of a lover can put its object in a prison. Did I do that? "Just go *away*!" I still wake to hear you say that. Exasperated, in anger, in despair, vehement pleading. "Oh! Just go *away*!" But often, almost always, if I waited a while, you relented and held out your hand. Which was the truth? The words or the outstretched fingertips?

I want to write down what we did so that you know what it was and what it meant for me. I have a conventional squeamishness about this but I must tell you so that you know that the strength of it is still there. I read that it is thought impossible to write about sex without being pornographic or ridiculous. What I write cannot be pornographic because it happened between us and it happened in the name of the strongest sensation of giving I shall ever know. As to being ridiculous – well, to someone who has been hooted down a main street by town yobbos and cautioned publicly for drunkenness (admitted) by a chit of a local policeman, the sense of the ridiculous is blunted. Perhaps those who find it ridiculous have never experienced it. Perhaps they are in that category of people whose background has made it inevitable that they laugh at deep feelings or are forced to undercut them to camouflage their own lack of them. So let it seem ridiculous. All I know is that this is what happened.

Remember this:

The summer of '89 was one of the hottest in memory. I had thought about the Lake District in various ways – as an escape, as a hobby, as the natural phenomenon on my doorstep, as a deep geological and literary mine, as a perfect walking space and, most mysteriously, as somewhere in which, very occasionally, I could 'lose' myself, go into a rich neutral of the mind and after some time re-emerge fortified. I have never seen it erotically. Until then I never saw that the Lake District lived and breathed sex.

But it did. The soft round fells were breasts, the broad valleys cleavages, the deep cuts vaginas, the warm cropped turf lay back in the sun like your bare pelt waiting to be disturbed. The trees, the tresses. More profound than such provocative references (you became very good at them) was the smell, the taste, the feel which came from the hot earth, from the warm rock, from the sky blazing on the blazing green, that this was a place of fecundity. To make love here was the condition of being alive. The land was there for nothing else.

Sometimes it was unbearable: although we were out of doors

there was a claustrophobic intimation of sexual activity, in plants, in the air, the wind, the rivers and lakes, and among all the creatures including us, the sense that we were only fully as we ought to be when we were making love, making others, expressing our faith in existence in that most primitive and decisive way: propagation. The only faith. Let the race, let all the various lives – of trees, of fowl and fish and insects and beasts and grasses – let it continue, please – Heaven? Or please ourselves. And to please ourselves is the whole answer if the pleasing produces more life. So those ghylls and fells, those becks and dales produced in me that summer the most violent and tranquil sense of what life is for. It is for itself. To grow and flourish and keep the account open. That is all there is hope for. But it is All. An awesome, almighty All. The Lake District then to me was like the great egg of myth, the Garden of Eden, the original African woman-mother of humankind, in its antiquity the big bang of fertility; walking there, existing there as we did on so many weekends was like being inside you, moving slowly there, feeling there was all the time for all the pleasure in the world.

What is superior to love and sex? Through the sex with you – which I want to detail but I have to build up my courage for that, have to wait until the last night train goes through and there is that gap in the dark where I dare write what would hitherto have mortified me – through making love to you I understood life. I understood it for myself. I have at last what might even be called a philosophy; or a view. I'll settle for a view.

It is the only time I have acted and willed something. As a young man I drifted with all the eternal convictions of youth – that life was forever, that opposition was surmountable, that by striving I would arrive in middle age on an island of achievement, a South Pacific paradise of all problems solved and there strum away the mature years in contentment.

Middle age brought the awareness, in fact the knowledge of my death. It was as if I woke up one morning – like a man in a Blues song – and knew I would die. Not then, but surely, and soon enough. Probably it is a chemical matter, the organism is just telling you – you're over the peak, now in the distance you can see the edge and you have to keep walking. For about two years I woke up with the same thoughts – measuring the length of time lived against a hypothetical time to come, totting up the figures, trying to fix the notion of death in an imagination which had not looked at it. There seemed to me to be a conspiracy. Nobody talked about it. Nobody appeared to worry much about it except the unmistakably ill. I read a little about the great civilisations of death – for instance the Egyptian – and while the organisation of society was repellent or baffling, the concern seemed to be more true to life or rather true to what was more important, death, than anything since. From then on everything in my life seemed to be either evasive action, wilful blindness or the dumb show of habit.

Until I fell in love with you, Bernadette. *Amor vincit omnia.* Even that. Now I realise that not only did I fall in love with you – (falling still, falling endlessly, like a man in deepest space, forever falling past meteors and stars and planets, whenever I think of you or see you I fall further, happily) – but with love itself. This is an embarrassing admission for a bank manager, even one who was considered rather bold in taking earliest possible retirement. What happened was like a religious revelation. I saw the light and the light was you and you were the light. But the light shone elsewhere. It showed me, as it shows me, that nothing can ever be as important as the twinned redeemers love and sex. The planet lives through love. And sex. You cannot leave out that tormented and eroded three letter word but if you are human you must bind it to love. The two together make what we have worth having. We as a race. There is little else. The evidence around us is too obviously appalling to chronicle; of course there are good people and good deeds – but that is not what we live by now. We live by degeneration and death. The only force which will take us forward is love.

But who can preach it? Who would dare to? It is a message which has been abused from the beginning. It evaporates on the tongue. The secret is to keep it to yourself. To act on it and know that you are never unique; others at this time will be feeling the same. They too will be acting on it. And maybe those independent actions will feed into the future. No! No more prophets. No more creeds. Let that be as it may. It is my life I am concerned with – and yours. You have turned your back on what we were, Bernadette. You have walked away from it and I fear you have blocked it out. Let me tell you what we did. If only I have the nerve not to flinch. I am nervous – that I may not write it well enough; that you may read it! that it will not be clinchingly detailed enough. In the detail is the truth.

It was as if you had been especially created for sex that summer. The jut of your hips, the innocently lascivious glance from a lowered face, the casual tugging of your skirt, the swing of your breasts – you were in the first great flood of a feeling which poured from you.

We possessed each other in those months. No part of our bodies was too sacred or too profane. You from your trauma, I from my amnesia, we burst on each other like storm and sun.

After that first weekend we went into the Lake District regularly. At best we would contrive to meet there on Friday evening and be back late on Sunday. I had enough credit with my wife to justify this. You had no ties. The ploys we used to sneak separately out of the town were, as we learnt, soon seen through but even if we had known that at the time we may well have continued to employ them. Deception can be spice to illicit love. Sometimes you could not join me until the Saturday. Once or twice you failed to make it. Once – when your mother was ill – you returned abruptly on the Saturday morning. But generally that was the pattern: two nights.

I chose to push into the Southern Lakes and to stay at expensive hotels. This, I calculated, would best bring me outside the range of people we knew, certainly outside their pocket. The very few who decided to holiday so near home and not drive back in the evening would seek out modest accommodation. Besides that, treating you well became part of it. Spending money became a coarse but highly visible way of saying how I valued you. If it put me at one with the tribesmen who layer their wives' necks with precious ornaments or the international *nouveaux riches* who do much the same then so be it. It was not only spending, it was wasting. I liked to exchange what had been such lovingly hoarded little rows of figures in the statements for a double bedroom at the Wordsworth Hotel where we could enjoy a swimming-pool, or a weekend at Sharrow Bay or Miller Howe where we were told we were eating of the very best. Previously I would have considered all such places to have been not only a waste of money but too much fuss. Now the more lavish the better. I even grew to enjoy room service.

We would arrive on the Friday at about seven or seven-thirty, book dinner for nine or later if we could, and go to bed. We would have seen each other through the week – though you forbade it from time to time – but that would only rarely have led to anything. Sometimes we managed in most delinquent circumstances, disturbing the peace in locations which I now revisit for a blush of pleasure, appraising the small back alley compulsion of our transactions; but mostly by Friday seven-thirty, we were hungry.

I trembled to meet you and was always fumble-fingered. The unopened cases went on the floor, we stood by the bed clinging to each other as if we had just been saved from drowning. The force of your own need and desire is something you cannot deny and I believe it could not have been faked. We twisted and tugged desperately at each other's buttons and zips, wanting to pause, wanting to go on, wanting to enjoy anticipation, wanting to be satiated. Most often you wore no bra and those wonderful breasts rode into my cupped hands and my mouth so firmly, so tenderly that there was a thud in my heart – to be so lucky. Your hands would rush nervously up and down my back, down my flanks as we tried to kiss, talk, embrace, undress and feel each other all in the same instant. Frantically we would separate and throw off clothes so fiercely that we often found rips and tears in them later. We would stand back and look at each other.

There you were. That wonderful female shape. Slim, vulnerable shoulders, deep breasts rising on the rather narrow body; flat stomach, sweet hard curve from ribs to thighs demanding a palm to sweep down it, shaking out your hair as you stared back. You were the first who has ever praised me; and the first who ever genuinely liked to reach down, hold me hard and tight until I was all but sickened with longing, and say how much you loved it.

We came together, do you remember, always tenderly, at

first standing, like a chivalric introduction to what was to be a voluptuous sensual battle? Just stood and kissed like children, simply, body to body, skin to skin, you slightly stirring against me, myself disregarding for those seconds the ram of sex aching below.

And then we would be on the bed and I touching you, hungry. Eyes closed, fingers inside you, reaching into the melting fluid rubbered silk – a relief map of mysteries – the eager clitoris, reeking of you, our tongues imitating the fingers, your hands gripping and stroking me but also careful not to excite too much. Already we knew each other. Knowing beyond talk; knowing in the blood. I loved you to be excited. The whole of my love-making to you was to make you happy, to make you come to the fullest completion. That was all I wanted. That *was* my love. My own intoxication was guaranteed in being with you. You touching me was a dream, your words (never again did you say 'fuck' although, perversely, once or twice I found myself saying it), the reality of you being there making love to me – that was more than anything I could have imagined. They are still the finest, the most profound, the most bloody exciting times of my life. My whole object was your pleasure. The greater your pleasure, the greater mine. The deeper your passion – eyes closed, head arched back so I reached up to kiss and lick your throat – the better, the finer for me. And so I would fuck you gently and then more strongly and finally thrust in hard and suddenly and let everything go. "Slam into me," you used to say, "how you just slam into me!" We would lie side by side which meant that I could hit – yes, hit – you harder for longer: then switch to be above you on propped arms, pulling right out and driving in again, hearing the slap of our bellies, percussive accompaniment urging us on and then you would flip over and the deepest thrusts of all while you crouched and half-goaded, half-checked me. During all those times I kept touching you, remember? – and when I could, took your nipple softly between my teeth so that every secretive part of you was seduced until you murmured words indistinguishable, and then "Like that" which grew to a moan, a croon, a song of arrival. And I too would come, our sounds and sweat and rhythm together. It was milk and honey: the Promised Land.

I still wonder how I could keep my sperm under control for so long. I became rather proud of it. It was easier later. For we would lie there for some time – (I wished I smoked) – have a shower, change for dinner – the red shoes – drink decent wine – Sancerre or Chablis to begin, St Emilion or Chateauneuf to follow and then a silly drink – Cointreau on the rocks or, more seriously, a malt – and move back to bed at about eleven-thirty. One time I actually sat down at my desk and began to work out equations between the quantity and quality of alcohol and the quantity and quality of activity. For, happily dulled by drink, it was perhaps easier to understand how the love-making could go on sometimes for a couple of hours. (I *did* keep an account of the time. Partly because I wanted to be impressed by us, partly because I have the bad habit of keeping accounts of anything which can be accounted for.) That was understandable. But that very first time – especially when I had spent what seemed the whole of Friday straining for you – well, the only way I can account for it is to go back to what I have already written. As it defies physiology it must be explained by psychology and the explanation has to be that I wanted you to be happy, you to be served more than anything else and was not only prepared but in some deep, unaccountable way, able to subdue what my conscious and, I would have sworn, my unconscious, most wanted. I dwell on this to tell you how complete the grip of my love for you was, what drove it was my wish, will, for your happiness.

For in that happiness I saw your brutal past erased. In the happiness I saw you glow with peace. Out of that happiness I knew a life could come different from and better than any you had thought possible.

In our mildly drunken state after dinner we would rummage about each other's bodies with a shameless curiosity I found heartbreakingly tender. There would still be bouts of passion when we seemed to be fighting each other as much as loving each other but that would not be the tone of those hours. That would be the quiet rhythm of a long coupling – you above me often as not letting your hair sweep over my face, giving me images of desire instantly satisfied as my mouth reached up for your breast or I trod my fingers down your spine until you said

"Yes, yes". Or we would lie side by side, me just resting in you, and talk about the future we could have – you were much sterner than I was about that and said you did not want to hear of it, although I noticed that you were not entirely loath to creep back to it. Just lying there, your legs curled around my waist, looking down at ourselves locked together. Now wanton, now virginal, Magdalene Madonna.

The third act and, in many ways, the most powerful, was in the mornings. Usually at about six. I would wake up huge. You, who never slept well, would be hovering beside me – as often as not you had woken me up though you always denied it. (Why?) We would sink into each other as if this was the last time. As if the dawn proclaimed not a beginning but an imminent ending. It was silent, relentless, always going as hard as we could – you sliding on to the floor so that it would be harder, clinging to me so that I was virtually holding you clear as the blows, they felt like blows, pummelled you. And you bucked and wrenched back until sometimes I felt I would be literally thrown off. Then standing, you bent over and me holding you open, and sometimes the strange (shameful) intriguing sight of our mirrored selves limbs and bodies wrapped around each other. Or you would lie flat and straight as a nun as I plunged into you – this time – all contrary to the others – wanting it to be over, wanting to finish it because there was something so raw, so mechanical about it, as if the love we knew had been worn away the previous evening, worn away before dinner, through the amorous meal and after-wards in the tenderness, leaving little else but the possessive drive of a compulsion. They were savage, those mornings, and whenever they ended I thought that we had only just got through. But they mattered: they were the anvil, the need. We would pull away from each other, sweat-soaked, silent.

But later in the day they would return to my mind – as they do now, as they do in agitation or occasionally in consolation during so many nights here – and through memory their harsh-ness finally achieved lovingness.

If that was the pattern there were tantalising exceptions. Remember the Friday you said "I've brought something for you"? You would not tell me what it was and I still was unaware when, unusually, you darted into the bathroom when we reached

our room. (By then we were blasé about checking in: no receptionist could daunt us; case-hardened.) "Here," you announced
as you stepped out in the skimpiest set of pink underwear –
salmon encasing your legs, rippling in lace lines across your
breasts, not quite covering that dark auburn bush. You twirled
around and laughed, but not at me; not at that curious and
questionable desire on the part of men to see women seductively
half-dressed – no, you were laughing, I think, because of the
pleasure you thought you were giving me. As indeed you were,
although by then the closeness of our bodies was so imprinted
on my mind that even the prettiest sexiest pink was as much an
impediment as a tease.

Fortunate man. But you must have been so relaxed with me
at that moment – do you see? – you must have felt so near. And
age? The difficulties of my circumstances, your own doubts
and inhibitions – all were far away by then. Those nights and
mornings, those gamey gestures, those mad, rough quick takes
in near-public corners – that was also us, Bernadette. Can you
find that again? Can anyone love you as I do? And – please think
about this – can you yourself love and be as loved? What would
you (do you?) feel like going through the same . . . how *could*
you . . . ? It does not bear thinking about except that you cannot
ignore it. You were there – heart, body, mind and, if there is a
soul, soul too. There was no hiding. There was no lying. You
gave yourself absolutely. You cannot do that again. Can you?
Please God, no. Is it possible to take that back? Is it possible
to live wholly with anyone except the person to whom you have
freely and entirely given all you have?

More than all that – for me, but this could be vanity – is that
we were then equal. The only talk of age was banter – to dismiss
its relevance. We swore it did not matter – nor did it. What we
had was most timeless of all – the present. We merged into one.
How fast the clichés come true in love! We were 'made for each
other' we said. How else to explain that we moved to each
other's gossamer touch, that we knew how to give pleasure
without question and knew we *had* given it without post-
mortems? Equal in what we brought to each other, equal in what
we took and what we gave. And it could go on, Bernadette.
That knowing of each other, that full fairness before each other

is as important as your showing and giving me all and my returning it.

What I want to write now is 'Thank you'. Love conquered age, conquered the grip of death. I never knew I could make love like that. I never thought there was love-making like that. For all I know it goes on all the time all over the place but it was foreign to me. You made me proud of myself, in a stupid way, perhaps, but there was energy in that stupidity and the fury and the intricacy of those nights and mornings of sex gave me a life I had not had.

Everything changed. On the Saturdays and Sundays we would walk. I took you everywhere – Grasmoor was one of your favourites and you liked the far Western Fells, Blake, the other side of Ennerdale and the hills above Loweswater and Crummock – we walked the tops that summer and the new boots soon became old soldiers. The landscape I had seen and walked became the mirror of our erotic life. Nothing I saw was ordinary. I felt like the first poets are said to have felt, as if I had stumbled on a paradise, except that for them the Garden of Eden was the place, for me it was you, you were the place. I cannot explain it more accurately and I do not want to rhapsodise forever. Your body, your sex, the smell of you on my fingers, the salt feel of your perspiring skin against mine, the knowledge of your breasts – all this made the place so vivid – because it became you – that the days were days of life.

So, Bernadette, the summer of '89. Until one Saturday evening, when you had to go back home. I had decided to stay on in the hotel. You had persuaded me that there was no point in my coming back with you, in fact I would be a positive nuisance! There was a lecture advertised, open to the public, in what was described as the Conference Room in the hotel's basement. This lecture was part of a Wordsworth Summer Conference and normally I would have thought it a little above me. But we had been reading some of our Lakeland Romantics and the speaker was a literary politician whom I had often seen and generally enjoyed on television. The good weather appeared to have broken. I had no urge to go out to a pub without you. I was looking for something to fill in the time and as this promised to last no more than an hour and a half I felt I

could risk it. Besides, the title beguiled me. 'Hazlitt In Love'.
Of Hazlitt I had only a rather vague notion: but anyone 'in love'
intrigued me.

I paid my £2.50 and went in. When I came out, our lives had
changed utterly: ruined.

THIRTEEN

There were well over a hundred in the room – the majority from abroad, as I was to learn at the coffee break, Americans and Canadians predominating, a few Japanese. The speaker rambled a little, but intriguingly, and I remember thinking that there could have been worse ways to spend an evening. His central argument, when he let you see it, was, I think, that Hazlitt's many and, from his quotations, vicious critics were all politically inspired – that is to say they did not like his politics and took it out on his writing. He added that much the same had happened to Wordsworth at the outset and to Shelley throughout his life. All criticism is basically political, he said. I was wondering what the lecture's title 'Hazlitt In Love' had to do with all this when he suddenly slid into a description of a curious love affair which Hazlitt, then a forty-two-year-old essayist and critic and man of letters almost two hundred years ago, had with the young teenage daughter of a lodging-house keeper in London.

According to the speaker this hopelessly erotic intoxication had (a) not interfered with the quality of his work but (b) exposed him to ridicule and given his exhausted political opponents just the ammunition they needed to open fire on him again. Which they did. Even now over the centuries we all winced at the brutality of the assault as he read out the reviews. But the speaker's point seemed to be that Hazlitt had brought the reaction on himself by publishing a book on the love affair – *Liber Amoris* (the Book of Love) or the *New Pygmalion*. Had this book not been published – for though it was anonymous, everyone knew it was Hazlitt since he had talked of nothing else around town for eighteen months – then he would have escaped the slaughter with benevolent consequences for his future

literary prospects and personal happiness. There was much else
but this was enough for me to absorb.

Although I did not then know enough about the subject to
comment on the content, of one thing I was sure. If Hazlitt's
obsessive love affair was as consuming as the speaker hinted
(he was reluctant to go into much detail) and if it was balked,
then he *had* to talk about it and as a writer he would surely write
about it. If only for the relief. If only to tell the world "Look,
this has happened to me! This also is what I am!" I feel that
about you – which is another reason why I made myself write
about our love-making (though it still falls far short of the reality).
I wanted to show what new continent had appeared in my world
– and even if it has been said ten thousand times, ten million
times before it has not been said by me. So for our political
speaker to censure Hazlitt for publication was for him not to
understand the need to cry out, even to boast, to declare to the
world "Look what there *is*! Look what I have found."

What happened in the basement Conference Room of the
Prince of Wales Hotel which changed me and ruined us was the
quotation of a single paragraph which I subsequently looked up
– when I became a Conan Doyle to Hazlitt: here it is.

"I do not think that what is called *love at first sight* is so great
an absurdity as it is sometimes imagined to be," Hazlitt wrote.
"We generally make up our minds beforehand to the sort of
person we should like, grave or gay, black, brown or fair: with
golden tresses or with raven locks; and when we meet with a
complete example of the qualities we admire, the bargain is
struck. We have never seen anything to come near our newly
discovered goddess before, but she is what we have all our lives
been looking for. The idol we fall down and worship is an image
familiar to our minds. It has been present to our waking thoughts,
it has haunted us in our dreams like some fairy vision."

That statement went home like a bolt. It was true to my
experience. This man spoke my mind. Suddenly I had a friend.
It was as if I had found someone I could confide in although of
course it was to be he who confided in me. Immediately I
thought – if he is like me in this – what about the rest? Obviously
'love at first sight' was a notion I had heard of in songs and
novels ever since I could remember – but it was this man saying

it – 'a scholar and a philosopher' as I discovered he liked to call himself – and being interpreted by a political figure I admired in company I could respect – the total effect completely seduced me. Certainly that summer I was in a mood to be seduced. I wanted to know more about this man's love affair.

The book itself – *Liber Amoris* – was on sale and so was a biography of Hazlitt. I bought both at the end of the talk and without staying to thank the speaker, all but ran up to my room (which had the previous night been *our* room) to read this book of love. I read and re-read until after five in the morning when I fell into a drunken nightmare.

When I began the book – which I read alongside the biography – I had a close and exhilarating sensation of companionship. He wrote that she (*she* was called Sarah) was "the only woman that ever made me think she loved me, and that feeling was so new to me, and so delicious, that 'it will never from my heart'". For that sentence alone he was again my friend. I thought – as all lovers tend towards egotism – that nobody in the world before me had experienced that precise thought. The insight clarified what I knew and it reinforced it. To an extent which cannot be measured, the fact that I knew that you loved me levered me out of what I had been and turned me into the man you knew. To be loved! Maybe you have known it in your family but I had never known it although I had known great affection and I had returned affection. But to be *loved*! However trampled on – by me as much as others – the word is harder than a diamond, and men and women will live and die for it if they ever find it. I found it in you.

I looked up William Hazlitt's background to see if it matched mine. There were enough correspondences. I read, later, some of his essays – far different from the *Liber Amoris* and, once I had got used to him, found a good deal to enjoy. (I have read more just lately. Reading is the only way I can staunch the wound – yes, it is a wound – of longing for you. The library has become a clinic.)

A second similarity was that he was already married when he met Sarah. So he knew that pain and complication too. He hoped to resolve that and some time on he began divorce proceedings.

Another similarity – his obsession began instantly. Within a week, he writes to Sarah: "You sat upon my knee, twined your arms about me, caressed me with every mark of tenderness consistent with modesty." Although these caresses appear to have been provocative and sensual, nothing further happened; but the caresses did go on for more than a year.

He wrote about her in words I wish I could have found for you. Words which in today's climate would be called extravagant but for me – as for him – were real. "Oh, I could see your face now – your mouth, full of suppressed sensibility, your downcast eyes, the soft blush upon that cheek . . . thou art heavenly fair, my love." (It seems, in truth, that she was not, but that is of no importance to the case.)

He praises her restraint, although it frustrates him greatly. He loves her pure but, I would guess, longs for her to be wanton. He applies all his forty-two years of intellect and study to her and yet they count for a milligram beside the ton of pleasure he found in simply having her on his knee for hours on end and just holding her by the waist.

But most of all – "the only woman that ever made me think she loved me". I felt vindicated. Perhaps there was a little intellectual snobbery in it. I left school at sixteen after 'O' Levels with results that could have taken me into the Sixth Form and, the Headmaster said, promised at least a fair crack at a university. But my poor mother's condition made it imperative that I leave school, and the bank gave us all the security we needed. I would look back and speculate on what might have happened. It would have been a fine life, that of a scholar. I've always read a great deal. Hazlitt appeared as a man of learning, a literary master, a man of thought, a man to be respected. That was a small but, I will admit, important element in my sense of being vindicated. I rang room service for a bottle of beer. I remember wanting to telephone you, to let you in on this glorious coincidence. But of course you had no phone. A habit you have not broken to this day! I marked in pencil the passages I would read to you.

Perhaps I took a shower before the beer arrived. I have only a foggy memory of what I did, a clear, bitterly clear, remembrance of what I read. When I wrote earlier of our behaviour in the hotels, I put down about a twentieth, perhaps even a hundredth of what I can recall. In memory I can take us through the doors of any of them step by step at will. It is, when I try to sleep, my sole consolation and perhaps my sanity. What I wrote of our love-making was a crude approximation: by taking thought I can recreate hours of those wild intimacies. But for the few hours of which I write now, hours which changed my life – I have nothing but a blank rush, an avalanche of panic.

Once, when I was about eight or nine, an uncle who now and then came to see us on a Sunday took me out onto our tiny lawn. He began to tickle me – I was very ticklish and easily made helpless. He would not stop. Even as I write this now, I can transplant myself over the forty-five intervening years and call up the terror of desperation I felt as I tried to make him stop. My cries became squeals. My laughter became hysteria. My heart grew hotter and hotter. Black flashes fled across my brain and saliva began to spurt from my mouth. I screamed like a pig with the knife at its throat. It was my mother who opened the window and told him to stop. I shook and trembled as if I had been in a terrible accident.

That was how I felt on that night.

For I read on and I discovered distrust. How I wished I had never picked up the book! Yet I could not stop!

Hazlitt began to distrust Sarah. He questioned why she would not do more than sit on his knee, why she suddenly withdrew even that favour, why she would inexplicably fail to come to his room – to bring him breakfast or whatever – often for days on end. He challenged her that she had another lover. She denied it although she admitted that she had loved someone once – a couple of years before – but he was too good for her and nothing had come of it save for her broken heart. Between these accusations, Hazlitt rushed back to compliment her and blame himself for wrongly interpreting her answers and her actions, but soon he was off again on the interrogation. When he went to Scotland to get a divorce she failed to write to him for weeks on end and when she did manage a note it was cold and formal. The man was in despair. In a state of madness he encouraged one of his friends to go and 'test' her: to take rooms at the lodging-house and see if she showed to him the easy favours she had so immediately shown to Hazlitt. Was she just a lodging-house flirt? Was she playing a particularly cruel game with him? (Overheard conversation suggested a lewdness and cynicism which ran altogether counter to her maidenish protestations.) His doubts and suspicions were so strongly and consistently diverted by her that he did not know what to think, of her, of himself, of the feelings he had. Though a man of great pride he confided to several friends what seemed to everyone but himself a ridiculous condition. And he confided his suspicions.

They were well founded. She *had* betrayed him.

Soon after meeting Hazlitt, she had met another lodger – Tomkins – and begun an equal or more intense or advanced flirtation with him.

Hazlitt's sense of alarm and insecurity was based on her alarming unreliability. She had deceived him, lied to him and double-crossed him.

But I had identified my – our – case with him, with theirs. What madness let me do that? I had thought I had found a friend and instead he turned me against you.

He had spoken for me. There was no way in which I could just turn off his voice or his influence. He continues to speak for me.

A rush of doubts and fears swarmed to my mind, choking it. Perhaps they had been accumulating over the months and needed only a trigger to release them. But perhaps not. I have brooded on this for a long time and I think not. I believe that Hazlitt's book created them. Having captured me he did as he liked with me. Or – put another way – I had surrendered happily to his superiority in describing what both he and I had so wonderfully experienced and I had no defence at all when the story changed. I read on, and on. I referred to the biography in the hope that some of *Liber Amoris* might be fiction and the real thing would give me hope. None. I had put myself in his hands and in his mind and he had led me into a swamp whose treacherous ground dragged down both of us.

For, immediately, I am ashamed to admit – but either you will value this for the truth of its confession or not at all – a throb of questions invaded my head. Where were you at that minute?

Why did you *have* to leave? And those other sudden departures
– could there be a pattern to them? When we were in the town
and you forbade me to see you on certain days – why was that?
And much earlier – the trip to Blackpool – was that entirely
innocent? Then – and so swiftly! – I attacked a very foundation
of what was between us – your letter. Was that the truth or
was it a very clever document designed to meet apprehensions
you had shrewdly guessed that I had? Your intuition is very
strong. Perhaps, I thought, in that wretched state, you had
sniffed out my worries and the letter was the answer. But then
why did you want to be with me? You enjoyed the talking, I
knew that; and the love-making, that could scarcely be faked;
and the places we went to, you said; the way we lived, the way
I promised you how we could live. But what was the *real*
attraction I held? If any. Or was I just a temporarily convenient
'boyfriend', even – remembering your mother's mercenary
nature – a speculation?

Dreadful, second-rate, disgraceful suspicions flooded in and I
could not close the gates. I could not channel them out. Within
a few hours they had saturated my mind. I tried to order them
away. I sat up in bed, like one demented, and said, aloud, "Go
away! *Go away*!" This may have been thanks to the whisky. I
called the night porter and ordered whisky: he brought me a
selection of miniatures – about half a dozen – and I bought and
drank all of them. I trace my addiction to whisky back to that
night.

My peace was destroyed.

The sleep, late and troubled, took me into mid-morning when
I woke up with a sore head, a parched throat, and the sensation
that I had to carry myself most delicately balanced to the
bathroom or brain fluid would tilt too heavily to one side of the
skull, eyeballs might be forced out, the shooting pains across
the forehead might attack even more sharply. Even so I was
out of the hotel in a few minutes and on my way back to the
town.

I went first to the pub where the Kennedys assembled for
quiet conversation and a chewing over the Saturday night's
adventures. You were not there. Big Joe – of whom I had by
then become genuinely fond – he wanted to take me poaching

with him – insisted on buying me the 'hair of the dog' and I admit that it made me feel much steadier.

I had never been in your house but I had contrived to pass by more than once and so it was without difficulty that I manoeuvred through the estate to your front door. Your mother was understandably surly (later explained by a rambling story about some family disagreement the previous night) and told me that she had 'no idea' where you were. "If anything," she added, "she should be with you." But hadn't your mother's illness been your excuse?

Imagine what I then felt! If only you had been there on that Sunday you could have caught the fever in its beginnings and subdued it, scalded it out of me. Without you it grew unchecked, feeding on itself. In that one day it became as savage a poison as the first impact of my love for you. The two battled it out and I did indeed – as you remember? – fall ill. Perhaps it was due to hovering around the town on what turned into a chilly and rainy afternoon. I was certainly shivering when I finally went home at about ten p.m.

Unusually, Angela was up. She insisted on making me a hot drink even though all I wanted was to go to bed, to get the night over with so that I could see you the next day and hear you quell those horrible doubts which tolled across my brain like the bells of doom. I put whisky in the hot drink and the combination – together, I think, with Anadin – eventually sent me to sleep.

Unhappily, the cold had bitten in. I woke up weak and sweating. I tried to get up but Angela – with uncharacteristic decisiveness, called Geoffrey – Dr Deans – who told me that I would be unable to walk for more than a few yards until the fever abated. (As soon as he left, when Angela's back was turned, I tried to prove him wrong and failed.)

So I was confined to bed for those few days, my body burning but as nothing compared with the burning inside my head. The questions stung and stung me. The suspicions rose like bats in a deep cave. The fear shuddered through me like a deep earth spasm. Were you faithful? Did you really love me? Would you ever marry me? Could you rid me of those terrible thoughts which were destroying the marvel, the wonder of what we had? I needed you and you were only a few hundred yards away but you could have been at the end of the world. The physical fever slackened but not the mental agony. Yes, I will even use a word as strong as that: agony. Sometimes I even whimpered for you, whimpered like a dog.

By the time I was fit enough to walk down the town and contact you, the poison had worked its way through all my defences.

Liber Amoris. The truth was that she *had* betrayed him.

FOURTEEN

Perversely I drove to the place where we had first made love. Was I hoping that the good energy of the place would annul the bad energy which I felt working up in me, masticating on me like a medieval goblin? Was it because I hoped the coincidence of place might split the atom of truth as I faced you with accusations of infidelity on the spot where my own first infidelity had occurred? Or was it even more mysterious than that, a compulsion I could not divine?

Over these last months among other reading I have been looking at psychic phenomena – from empathy and premonition to the skills lost to us but still, they say, to some degree extant in the Kalahari Desert or among the Aborigines. I am more and more inclined to believe those who hold that once upon a time we had highly developed instincts now replaced by writing, by libraries, by computers, by all the strange systems of language. But in extremis, or in a few individuals, these or some of these powers reappear like old volcanoes which are never quite extinct, old springs which one day 'miraculously' yield up fresh water again.

Of course this conclusion could be a condition of spending too much time alone, with books, thinking of you! Yet I think not. There are many other worlds we know nothing of until we are forced to meet them. External worlds of knowledge, scientific knowledge, universes of facts and objects outside imagination until they are presented to us, and internal worlds of dreams and intuitions, unknown until circumstances force them on us. Which is why I can think this letter is a form of spell. It is as if I am chanting around a cauldron! Carefully placing the ingredients in the boiling of my unabated love for you. Willing it to get me what I want. What I had. What, I am sure, you too want; still. (I saw you yesterday down in the park. You were pushing your niece on the small swings. You did not see me. I was in the shelter. I don't know what impulse had taken me down there but it was not calculated and so I do not feel that I have broken my word. I could see you clearly some of the time. You looked tired and sad, still lovely – oh! Still lovely – but tired, tired arms pushing the swing, sad expression, forlorn, lost. I wanted to come across and hold you and comfort you but you would have ordered me away, sent me away for ever, isn't that so? Or am I right in still believing that you could still love me?)

That evening you were as bouncy as I had ever known you. You positively frolicked! Tickled me as I was driving. Made fun of my cold – 'old age creeping on fast' – but were sympathetic in those quick warm dabs of understanding which never failed to touch and heal me. You chattered on about work, doing rather good imitations of the others in Christopher's office. You caught his pipe-sucking pomposity to a T. You wore a new dress – a navy-blue, white-hooped affair which rode up way over your knees and at one point, just as we were approaching a tricky right-hand turn onto Caldbeck Common, you grabbed my left hand and thrust it between your thighs, clamping it tightly, laughing loud and hard as I, hesitating to be released from such sweet pressure, struggled with the steering-wheel and swerved dangerously across the road.

It was a placid late summer evening. We got out to stroll and you smiled and pointed up the hill towards the 'place'. The light was clear and soft. The nearby Skiddaw fells in bare brown pelt, so clear; further down, into Borrowdale, the tops smoking with light greyish clouds just tinting to mauve as the sun began its descent over the Solway. A few sheep, a scattering of wild ponies, sound of a tractor throbbing in the distance, a huge scoop of peace in a landscape carved by ice, stripped by men, in some way intact. The heather beginning to find a lush purple, shadows light in the gulleys, the tip of Bassenthwaite Lake catching the falling sun: that inexplicable Lake District sense of significance and insignificance simultaneously, of tranquillity.

And I see you there as clearly as I see this pen between my fingers. However often I describe you I can never get it right enough. Just as the landscape painters up here were – I read –

tested and exasperated by the rapidly changing weather as the winds whipped across the sea and soared up to the crest of the fells – so am I by your lovely, witty face, the grey shards in your black eyes, that beauty spot you hated just at the corner of your eye – I can reach out and touch it – the deep black and thick strength of hair, the sweet gobbling lips, the free and unaware enticement of your posture – legs braced apart like a boy on a ship, waist wasp tight, breasts soft and unbound – you are there, now, in my mind's eye – the last time I saw you totally happy with me. That is what I must find again.

What was it that drove me to destroy that moment? And in destroying that moment, destroy everything? Who can account for the self-destructiveness of destructiveness? I think am reasonably intelligent. I knew that to challenge you would antagonise you and might well alienate you. I knew that there was only the remotest chance that I would get satisfaction. I knew that I was on course to destroy the finest, most momentous thing that had ever happened to me and yet *I could not stop myself*! Is this an essential part of us too? and does it increase the more we love? Where did it come from? Just from reading the book? Was that sufficient explanation? I must have been ready for it or how had the spirit of William Hazlitt (died 1830) entered and enslaved mine? Even if I had known I could not have stopped myself.

"Isn't it beautiful?" you said, taking the first word and being unashamed in a weary world to express your wonder at the view. I loved you for that too. "Who would ever want to live anywhere else?" You were near me; you held on to my arm and nuzzled into me as we stood in that calm evening as if on the deck of a ship and gazed out at that ocean of fells and valleys, sky, cloud, shadow and the slowly gathering colours of sunset. "And it's you, you know." You tugged my arm and stood on tiptoe to reach up and kiss my cheek. "You've introduced me to all of this. I would never have got here on my own."

You rested your head on my shoulder.

Why did I have to speak? I tried to swallow it down; I swallowed hard as if to block nausea. I fought with all my might to divert, to cheat, to kill off this vile worm which crawled out of my intestines and up on to my tongue. But I was beaten.

"Where were you last Sunday? I looked everywhere. Where were you?"

You paused and then pulled away. My tone had been much harsher and more accusing than I had intended. Indeed there was real bitterness in it. I could not stop; the abscess was lanced.

"And three weeks ago – when you said you had to get back on the Saturday night to see your mother – why couldn't one of your sisters have seen to your mother? And isn't it rather unlikely that she would want you in particular around her? You're not even her favourite. And those days when you tell me I must on no account come down the street to see you. Why *is* that? Are you seeing someone else? Is that what it is? And those Saturdays. Are they because you are seeing someone else? Saturday *is* the big night, isn't it?"

You were standing well apart from me by now and I will never forget your expression but I will never be able to read it, either. Contempt? Sorrow? Shock? Anger? Hurt? All five? But at that moment I saw it only as the expression of somebody who had been caught out. Oh! Even if I could have stopped there! Perhaps over weeks or months reparation could have been made. But I went on!

"And your letter. Do I believe that? Was there *really* such a lodger? Or was it just somebody whose money your mother fancied? And are you playing the same game with me now?"

You looked stunned. Or were you acting the look? In my crazed state I did not know – oh! Forgive me Bernadette – I was weak from a fever, I had been taken over by the mind and the life of another man – a dead man – to whom I had been too open and what I was saying was no more than – Do you really mean it? Do you really care for me? Prove your love by surmounting this horrible obstacle. Perhaps I was setting you tests – in some unconscious way (but remember how deeply I feel, how forces I do not understand took over and can still take over) – they set tests in the legends and once through them people were stronger. There is that possibility.

But not then. You simply shook your head. I had envisaged chit-chat, question and answer such as you got in *Liber Amoris* but the force of my bilious suspicion, which surprised me in its intensity, silenced you. You looked at me; you stared at me as if you wanted to imprint the image on the screen of your mind and then you turned and walked away.

Fool that I was I watched you go. I let you go and in some terrible twisted way I thought – that proves it! There was – momentarily – a degree of satisfaction as if I had smoked you out and could see in your flight how right I had been. Fool! That was the devil's laugh.

I blundered over to the car and found that my hands were shaking so badly I could not put in the key. I wound down the window and took some deep breaths. The sky, I remember, had turned scarlet as the clouds sucked the last blood out of the sun. When I finally started up you had disappeared from view and then began the intolerable business of tracking you. You refused to keep to the road. I would park and call out for you but you never looked back. I would drive to cut you off. When you saw me coming you would tack away. I took the car onto the Common and bounced it so badly I reached the road again only with great difficulty. And had lost you again. As the sun finally set and dusk crept down the hillside I feared that I would never find you. Pointless to tell you how I cursed myself! How ashamed I was. Pointless partly because there is no excuse and partly because – as you know – the compulsion and the fear were still there! Finally I almost ran you over. It was nearly dark. You were persuaded to come into the car where you huddled, as far away from me as you could, arms tightly folded, eyes fixed on the floor, cheeks, I saw, glistening with tears.

"I'm sorry. I don't know why I did it. I've been ill. It's madness. Of course I don't suspect you of anything . . . Just . . . Please tell me where you were on Sunday. I don't know why but it's got under my skin and I have to know. Tell me that and then please, please try to forget the rest. It was horrible. It wasn't me. You know me. That wasn't me. Was it?"

God knows why but after a pause you were prepared to give me a chance. I knew at the time how understanding you were; now I look back and think you were even better than that, you were forgiving.

"There's a sister," you said, "or she may not be a sister – nobody's ever come out and really said. Anyway . . ." You

seemed to dig your hands deeper under your arms, sink your
face further down. I drove very slowly along the unfenced road
across the Common. "Anyway, she's not quite right. She was
born not quite right – again, nobody tells you why; it's madden-
ing. Spina bifida, very like. She's lovely, though. She lives with
an aunty of mine at . . ." you mentioned a small seaside town a
few miles away "and I go and see her as often as I can. I seem
to have a knack of getting on well with her. She's been restless
these last few months and she's asked for me a lot. I put her
off – to be with you – but sometimes I just had to go. Once or
twice when I've been with you it's just built up and built up and
I've felt more and more selfish and I've had to go."

"Why didn't you tell me?"

"I don't know."

I stopped the car and we looked out at the dusk, the fells now
dark velvet smothered outlines, a mass on the landscape. What
could I say . . . ? Not only had I suspected you quite mistakenly
and on the word of a man dead for almost two centuries, but I
had spoken those vile words which could never be recalled
and met with an explanation so sane and so good, that my
valuation of your character rose up and went off the graph. And
then:

"Why didn't you tell me about her before?" I heard myself
repeating, harshly this time.

"I've told you. I don't know. Perhaps I was ashamed of her
in some way."

"But you can't be. Not with what you do for her. That's your
family – not you."

"Some things are catching."

"But how did you know she'd suddenly need to see you? I
just ask . . ."

"I'd have talked to her through the week."

"Does she have a phone?"

"Yes."

"So you phone from the office?"

"Yes."

"And you would put her off – I'm just asking – but later feel
guilty and find it unbearable and have to leave me?"

"Yes."

"I understand that," I said. And my voice added, "But why do you avoid me through the week?"

"I don't avoid you."

"Yes you do – but let's not talk about that. Why do you tell me not to come down into the town on certain days? What are you doing then?"

"Nothing."

"You must be doing something."

"Whatever."

"Why can't you tell me? Is there someone else you see?"

"Will you take me back please."

"There's probably a perfectly reasonable explanation . . ."

"If you don't start the car I'll get out and walk."

"Why can't you tell me?"

You opened the car door. I switched on the engine.

Again we drove along in silence. After that explanation about your 'sister' how could I be so crass?

"I'm sorry."

"I know." You sounded weary.

"I don't know what got into me."

"What has?"

"You'll laugh."

"Go on. Why are you asking me all these questions?"

I tried to explain to you about the lecture and *Liber Amoris* and Hazlitt 'speaking' for me in the feelings he had for Sarah and then taking me down this treacherous road of suspicion. Badly as I may have explained it to you earlier in this document, it is nothing like the fumble-tongued mess I made of it while spinning out the drive back across the Common.

"You mean because he suspected her – in this book – you suspect *me*?"

The answer, in a way, was "yes". But I had not the nerve to give it.

"I don't believe it," you murmured, "I just don't believe it." You gave a laugh: like a cackle. A sound I had never before heard from you. It was unsettling.

We drove on and into the town and as I took you down to your house in a silence which had the nature of a truce I tried – with all my might, Bernadette – to stop myself from saying what was pressing at my lips. Like a devil determined to be exorcised – or determined to come out and cause havoc? Was something so jealous of what we had that it could not bear it?

We drew up and you waited. You were in a mood for a sort of reconciliation, I thought. You did not move towards me but when I put my arms around your shoulders you did not stiffen or shrug me away. Your body felt soft-boned, crushed in some way. For a few healing moments our heads rested against each other and there was a possibility of peace. Until I could no longer hold it back.

"What about your letter?" I asked. "Was that true?"

You moaned as if you had been winded, opened the car door and ran into your house.

I dared not follow.

What had I done?

I thought of the beauty spots: eight on the upper left arm; five on the right; of varying sizes and textures.

You vanished over the next few days. Christopher's solicitor's office had three exits (if you include – as I am sure you must have done – the door out of the basement back). You or your friends could always spot me outside on the street and so it would be quite easy for you to dodge out of the door I could not cover. And once out you could lose me in that old town centre.

You vanished.

I hung around the pub – enduring the continuous stare of the landlady who, I now comprehended, was mesmerised by my friendship with the Kennedys. You never showed up, of course, and none of your family, not even Big Joe, was forthcoming. To be fair to them, they did not appear particularly interested. It was not as if they were concealing anything from me – just that they were not very aware of your comings and goings.

On the Friday I became desperate and did what I had never done before: I rang Christopher.

"I need to get in touch with Bernadette Kennedy. Is she there?"

"Afraid not." He sucked on his pipe: I could swear to it! It was a most disapproving suck and he added, "I've been expecting a call from you on that subject."

"Have you?"

"I know you take an interest in the girl." There was a significant pause. I wanted to tell him to mind his own business but more than that I wanted to know where you were and keep this channel of communication open. "If truth be told," he continued, "there are one or two of us rather concerned about the interest you seem to be taking in her. Speaking as a friend, of course." In other words, it was all around the town. I had known that, I had seen that, but I had blocked it out. One thing at a time. But Christopher's smug dart reached its target and in my unbalanced state I put my hand over the mouthpiece of the telephone and cursed his nosey intriguing gossipy still life of a small-town mind. That done, I resumed.

"She's a very bright girl."

"Granted," said the pipe-man, "but not altogether reliable. We're not sure of her stamina over the long haul."

Which long haul? I wanted to seize him by the throat for this idle slander but quietened myself by imagining he was being skinned alive by a Gurkha.

"Christopher. I need to speak to her. Do you know where she is?"

"Have you tried her home?"

"Yes."

"The pubs? I hear she gets in the pubs – which is supposed to be quite natural these days – but for my money someone working in a job which carries the responsibility we carry should take jolly good care not to expose himself or herself to the dangers – I use the word advisedly – which could come from loose contacts – not necessarily of her own choosing – in public houses. There is also the matter of her family. One of them is up again in a fortnight –"

"I know."

"Oh. I didn't realise that you were quite as *au fait* with all the Kennedys. But my point is, how does it look when one member of the family is as it were against the law and another is there to uphold it?"

"You're not thinking of discriminating against her because of her brother, are you?"

"It has to be thought through."

"That would be disgraceful."

"Allow me to be the judge of that. In the matter of disgrace I need no lessons from you."

"So you don't know where she is?"

"I do not. She left early today – as she is fully entitled to do one Friday afternoon in three, as I believe you know."

"Sweet dreams."

"Pardon?"

"Never mind."

I did not trust myself to think about him any more; and yet his warnings – about the town gossip, and his threats – to you over your job, circulated around my mind and became part of the growing torment and the pressure.

I went in the pub that night and confronted both Joe and Theresa independently. Neither of them had any information. I then asked about your 'sister'. They looked blank (or brazen?) and confessed to no knowledge at all of such a being.

Of course they could have been blocking her out of their lives, hiding her away as you suggested. Yet their denial of her existence was so flat that once again the engine of suspicion began to growl. Was that another lie?

I spent the whole of Saturday at that seaside town. It was a blustery day, the waves throwing themselves desperately against the sea wall. If you were to take her out for a walk, then surely you would come here, I thought, across the green from the church, past the clump of pines to the little promenade where the sea air would be thought to be bracing. But you did not come.

I walked the streets but which door could I knock on? Whose help could I seek for a woman whose name I did not know? I thought of going to the Post Office to ask about disabled people but – fortunately perhaps – by the time I had formulated that idea, the Post Office was closed. I thought of the police but could not work out a plausible story. I stayed there from eight-thirty in the morning until nine-forty-five at night. By the end of it I was chilled stiff.

Yet I came back the next day at the same time and followed the same hopeless procedure.

It was when I got home that night that Angela finally spoke

up. She had prepared a supper and kept it hot in the oven. She made a large pot of tea. I noticed – through my own self-absorbed misery, that she moved restlessly around the kitchen in her quilted powder-blue dressing-gown.

She watched me eat and drink which I did in the manner of someone taking in fuel. Then, very tentatively, she told me that she had been in growing pain over the past few months, that she had not wanted to tell me – she could see how busy I was. But finally she had called in the doctor who had made her an appointment for an X-ray on the Monday. Would I drive her to the hospital?

To my eternal shame, my first thought was – at what time? Not at five-thirty because then I have to be outside your office to see you.

Midday, she offered, without my asking but as if answering my unspoken question.

She began to weep, splodgily, sniffingly, her face soon a crumpled contortion. I stood up, went over to her and put my arm around her by way of comfort. It was the first physical gesture, the first comforting move I had made towards her in weeks. Her crying increased, her sniffing grew louder, she pressed the back of my hand to her soft fatty wet cheeks and said "You're so good. You're so good."

This was so untrue that I could scarcely bear it. I had betrayed her, I had abandoned her emotionally. I now saw – I had always seen but refused to face it – that I had exposed her to shame and humiliation in the town. She was the part of my life I never brought to you; she was the third side of a triangle I had been too cowardly to admit to. Oh – I would, in time: a divorce would be instigated, arrangements would be made – but not yet, not while everything was so good between us, Bernadette. That had been my line and I would follow it again.

But Angela's part, Angela's story; the shadow to ours. We had walked without a shadow and that was unreal. Her grief and, bewilderingly, her gratitude bore in on me. I helped her, I believe, that night. I saw her to bed and stayed by her until she fell asleep. When I went into my study there was a large brown envelope on my desk. Her notes: her story.

Now you must know it.

FIFTEEN

My love,

You were the only one who never referred to my freckles
[it began]. Nobody else could resist. You could hardly
blame people – my face was practically overgrown with
them. When I was a girl I thought that they were a
terrible joke. I thought that they would just come off
one day if I washed them hard enough or if I said my
prayers every night or when I had my next birthday. If
anything they got worse in my adolescence. It was like
looking out at the world through a thicket. I imagined
people making remarks. I wanted to say 'Look, these
freckles are not me. I'm me. Underneath. The real me.'
But nobody could see the real me. And to be absolutely
honest nobody much wanted to. They say until you've
had a thing yourself – a stammer or a slipped disc –
you can't truly know what it's like. That applies to
freckles. And even when you meet a fellow sufferer you
avoid the subject like the plague; which is what it feels
like sometimes even though that might sound rather
exaggerated. You can't get used to it because you see
it every morning and every night when you brush your
teeth and wash your face. Always there. And make-up's
hopeless. Either you put on a mask like a circus clown
or you throw in the towel. I threw in the towel at sixteen.
Lipstick just about made it although my lips look like
old potato skins; mascara and eyebrow pencil smuggled
their way through; a touch of powder on the nose
where there was a particularly evil freckle which at one
stage, I was convinced, would turn into a wart; that
was my lot.

People expect you to be a certain type of person when you have freckles. You're supposed to be the girl next-door. The next-door to where I lived was half a mile away. They expect you to say 'gosh' and be this terrific sport, full of vim, bursting into laughter at the slightest hint of anything amusing. Freckled people who don't behave like that – and I did not – are thought to have something a bit wrong with them. No sense of humour. No 'go' in them. I always find people with 'go' a little wearing.

Apart from putting a bag over your head – which I thought of trying once or twice as a young girl – we didn't have 'teenagers' then, I was before them – you just had to get on with it. Even the usual comparisons were not a great help. It was better than being blind, I would say. But was it? I knew a blind girl and everybody was lovely to her. It helped I suppose that she was lovely-looking. But there was a contentment about her that I never felt. Better than having just one leg? Artificial legs were improving by the day. They could even bicycle with them now. Better than having a hare-lip? They could operate on that. No, stupidly, I settled on freckles as the worst of all disasters that could have befallen me.

You did not appear to notice them. You must have done but you never commented. No 'jovial' cracks but no hearty 'I *do* like freckles!' nonsense either. Later I thought that dealing with your mother had made you sensitive. You brought her with you to the town and everybody commented on how good you were to her, settled in that little house in William Street. I wish I'd seen her. Apart from anything else I was grateful to her for keeping you in the town. Usually, in those days, you were moved from bank to bank but they let you stay put on compassionate grounds.

We were all surprised that you wanted to. Mr Dawson said you were a 'rising star' and anybody could tell that, just looking at you. What a dashing and handsome young man you were! All of us thought that. I was going to write

'all the girls' but I wasn't much of a girl then: thirty when
you arrived, six years older than you. On the shelf.

I had sort of ruled marriage out. It wasn't just the
freckles. My mother and father on that farm were
very old-fashioned – they could even be called quaint.
They were quite old when I was born. He would never
invest in a tractor (mind you, this *was* the Forties and
Fifties): horses were good enough for his father before
him and so they were good enough for him! They were
very gentle people. I suppose you would call them
ignorant by today's standards. They were very
dyed-in-the-wool. I was a virgin – you didn't quite
believe that until you had to, did you? More than that,
though, I was terribly shy – not modern at all. With
that and the freckles I was always two laps behind in a
three-lap race.

I never felt shy with you. Whenever I worked
alongside you I felt as if I had been doing it all my life.
Because you know I fell in love with you at first sight.
People can. I did. Not that I told you or did anything
to spoil what we had. It never occurred to me – well, it
did, but only in day dreams – that I could have you
and so I made the best of what there was. I was the
first at the bank and, but for Mr Dawson, the last to
leave. It was far better than home.

It was the last time things were nice, the end of the
Fifties. Everybody thinks their past was golden but I know
that time was for me. And it helped that things were
nice. They hadn't knocked down half the town to build a
car park. There were not all that many cars – I suppose
that was the reason – and no supermarkets so shops
were shops and not warehouses. People seemed to have
more time to stop and talk on the street without worrying
that a twenty-four-wheel juggernaut would mow them
down. You could pick blackberries in hedges that ran into
the town and there were still horses about and men who
knew about them. I don't know – it was just nicer. Nice
was what people liked to be then. The churches hadn't
all emptied and schoolchildren were not allowed to

race about the town in gangs in their lunch break. There
was less money and that must have been difficult for
some but there was less greed and grasping as well. It
was slower then but somehow there was more to it. I
fitted in then.

You took to the place as if you had been born here. Look
at the tennis club. The best I ever managed was to stand and
watch for a few Saturday afternoons and then get roped in
to help with the sandwiches on a club day. You were
playing from the start. Everybody wanted to be your
partner. You made it look easy, never fussed, never
bothered if you won or lost. Sometimes I've seen you let
somebody win just to give them a leg up. It was perfection
watching you serve, in those little white shorts!

Your mother died quite suddenly and you took it hard.
Then you started to go away for weekends and I was
convinced you had a lady friend in another town. The
suspicion used to drive me crackers. I would start the
countdown on Saturday afternoon when we left the
bank and just knock off the hours until Monday morning.
I would make any old excuse to trail past William Street
to see if you had come back early. I found out the train
times and would make a point of being in the vicinity
when the evening train pulled in on a Sunday. If you
saw me you were unfailingly pleasant. You must have
suspected something but you never let on. It was
foolish I guess but I've heard of people doing more
foolish things on narrower grounds. I worshipped you.
I know it's blasphemous as well as unhealthy to worship
a human being but there we are. Others had their film
stars and pop stars and sporting heroes and idols of all
kinds – and husbands and boyfriends as well of course
– for me you were all of them wrapped up in one. I
honestly believe that I would have enjoyed a fair degree
of happiness if I had just been able to carry on working
with you and seeing you every day. Seeing you! Just
to see your face every day and hear you talk, that
pleasant twang of Derbyshire still perceptible, would have
done me.

The great stroke of luck was becoming your part-time
secretary when you – at the very young age (for those
times) of twenty-eight became deputy manager. It was
not much of an office but it had a door you could close
against everybody else. Once I was inside there with
my pad on my knee we were cut off. I was so terrified of
losing the job that I made some howlers. Do you
remember 'worried' with one 'r'? And 'temporary' with
a 'u'? My fingers would tremble when I sat down in front
of that old typewriter. You would just put a tiny pencil
mark through the offending letter and pass it back
without a word. I spent one whole weekend pulling myself
together and after that it went swimmingly.

I was only your part-time secretary of course. An
hour a day would be a long stint in that first year. Then
it began to build up. You can have no idea how much
that meant to me. When I was sitting there, opposite
you, listening to you trying to be fair to people – well,
I wouldn't have called the Queen my aunt, as my
mother used to say. You were so quick, and funny in a
quiet way. And looking at you – you were such a
good-looking man. Why did I never tell you that? Why
was I never able to say that to you? Only now. And I have
to write it because I could never speak it: not even now,
when there's this bothersome pain and, to be perfectly
honest, I have one or two glasses of whisky these days.
If only I could have told you so many things that I felt
– would it have made a difference?

Her question stopped my reading. *Would* it have made a difference? Already, just those few pages into her notes, I was seeing
a woman who was slightly, but perhaps crucially, different. It
was true that she was terribly shy. But how could her shyness
prevent her from saying what meant most to her – or so I asked
myself until I realised that I had been in the same boat. When
had I told *her* how much I cared for her? Of course I muttered
the usual 'I love you' – or I suppose I did. And I'm sure that
Angela responded in kind although again I cannot hear the words.
I wanted to tell her how sweet her expression was – she had

lovely grey eyes, the nicest smile, auburn hair so abundant and
it could glow like coal in a fire. But because of those freckles I
never dared refer to her looks. She was always so self-conscious
about them. They were very numerous. There may be other,
there may be many couples like us who cannot or will not say
what matters most. It can be very appealing, the unspoken, the
merest glance, the thoughtful unnoticed support, the darting
affection in an unbroken stream of attentiveness; and that is
what we had at our best. It seemed to work for Angela: for
some time I thought it worked for me. But I'm getting ahead of
her story.

Those three years were happier than ever I could have
imagined. Because you were such a desirable bachelor
and I was 'getting on to my forties' nobody suspected
my feelings (or if one or two of the girls did, they
never thought to take them seriously) and we could have
jogged along for long enough. You would go to a dance
now and then with another girl; and there was Celia
Strickland you partnered an awful lot one year at the
tennis club but she took up with Dennis Johnstone (dead
now) and so that danger passed. It was the closest
shave that I knew of although those mysterious weekend
trips recurred every so often and you have never admitted
what you did then. Not to this day!
   Father had died some years before and when Mother
fell ill I had to take leave to look after her. My brother
was off into Scotland on his own farm and there was
nobody else she wanted. I could not refuse of course
but I have to confess that I had a struggle. It is very
painful to admit this but I am setting down my version
if you like and I must not spare myself. I would have
preferred not to have gone home and looked after
Mother however disloyal and cold-hearted that sounds.
The thought that I would not see you for weeks and
maybe months – or even longer – was almost unbearable.
For what would happen if Mother's illness dragged on?
She was in her eighties and she seemed to be wasting
away but in her day she had been a strong working

woman and who knew how long she would hold out?

Mr Dawson was very understanding but when he explained that the leave could not be 'indefinite' my heart dropped into my boots. What if I could not resume work at the bank *at all*, for ever afterwards? You must have understood some of my unhappiness because you were very kind and made the letters extremely short in that last week. You hung back after we finished on the Saturday and asked if you could run me home – you had just got that little Ford – but I had my bike. You watched me go. I could have been setting off for Durham Gaol.

A few days after she left I grew restless. Mr Dawson gave me another girl who was pleasant and willing – though a bit too giggly and not very good at figures – but I began to realise that I was missing Angela. Over those three years we had become friends. Although she implies I made friends easily, I never made fast friends. Angela was the one I chewed the fat of the day with. Those little matters that need reassurance or adjustment, all those had been cleared through Angela and I missed her for that. She was also – I do not want to be ungallant but it's too late for rose-coloured spectacles – a very comforting presence: safe, discreet, warm, undemanding and with a mind of her own. That was refreshing. The tone of these notes should not mislead you. Angela was never afraid to speak out and even though she would soften an opinion she would never betray it.

Out of the blue one Saturday afternoon you came to the farm to see me.

That I can remember very clearly. I had cleaned the car and done my shopping. It was a clear coppery autumn day. I was oddly lonely in those few months following Mother's death. I decided to drive into the Lake District and find a farmhouse where I could have a good cream tea. (I thought of the Lake District as a cross between a spa and a retirement home in those days.) The route took me onto the Northern Fells and I

discovered – or had I known all along? – that I was near her
farm and I swung off down the long unmade road which led to
it.

It sits smack under a fell – good pasture fields to the north of
it, fell land to the south. She had talked about it a few times but
nothing had prepared me for the charm of the place. After her
father's death they had let out most of the pasture and all the
fell land and kept only a large paddock and the home field. The
paddock held three old cart-horses – Clydesdales – well past
their prime but still magnificent creatures who reminded you of
Piers Plowman and the massive guns being dragged to the Front
in the Great War. Her father had stipulated that they be well
looked after and even I, no horseman, could sense the satisfaction coming from the old beasts as they swung their long heavy
tails and wandered about thick grass which had never known
the application of anything but natural fertiliser.

In what I came to know as the home field were the three
cows – Buttercup, Daisy and Pansy – for all the world like plump
old dowagers, chewing the cud as if they were idling away the
time in gossip, there to provide them with milk enough for their
own needs – no great burden, no need for udder straining with
large-veined effort – and some left over for butter. The farmyard
was cobbled and along the barn wall leaned an old plough while
in another corner was the old hay-wain which could
have modelled for Constable. A few hens and geese owned
the territory and were undisturbed when Flash the
sheepdog trundled across as I got out of the car. Angela came
out of the stables where she had been tidying up. I will not
say that there were hayseeds in her hair and a straw between
her teeth but she looked the part. Baggy old corduroys, a
checked shirt, wellingtons. Her smile of welcome was memor-
able.

Inside the house – a late eighteenth-century stone-built
farmhouse – was even more quaint than outside. Much of the
furniture was dark oak – corner cupboards, chairs, a heavily
carved dresser, bedding chests – some of it made by her father's
uncles who had specialised in farm furniture. There were still
oil lamps on the tables even though electricity had arrived a year
or two before. The atmosphere was sober and dark but not

gloomy. It had the rich brown and black shadows of those Dutch paintings I saw when Angela and I went on a rather disappointing trip to Amsterdam (food-poisoning – unexpected in the Netherlands). Angela took me upstairs to see her mother who was propped up in bed against large flock pillows, starched white. She had the clearest complexion of any woman I have ever seen. Unblemished, snow-white, like her hair.

Before that afternoon, [Angela continued] the most exciting thing that had happened to my mother all year was the morning she counted twenty-seven Red Admirals on the buddleia outside her bedroom window. But I had talked about you of course and she must have guessed something of my feelings – although she never mentioned the subject. You were a great personage – an assistant bank manager *and* a friend from the town.

It was amazing watching you with her. Within half an hour you seemed to be nearer to her than I had ever been. Truth to tell I was always a little afraid of her. I had been closer to my father. Mother was very strict, very low church. I had never heard her laugh so much as she did that afternoon with you. Afterwards when I told you how good you were with her you just said "Practice". It was more than that. You were sympathetic to her. You didn't draw back or think of her as just an old nuisance. You really enjoyed her company. She would tell you things about her childhood – back before the turn of the century – and bring it to life in a way she had never done for me. Her childhood as far as I was concerned had been a very bruising struggle and it was held up as something to beat me about the head with: my life was a paradise of good fortune compared with hers. Even going off to work in the bank was seen as a privilege undreamed of. Never mind. We got on well enough. She had given all her real affection to my clever brother who had upped and married a woman with money in the Borders and got himself a fine spread near Kelso. He was a rare visitor which was rather unkind

as his two children were her only grandchildren and she
longed to see them. You made up for some of that.

That afternoon was the beginning of it, wasn't it?
Corduroys and all. The first kiss – just inside the
porch. And you tapped my nose with your index finger,
very lightly, on the worst freckle.

I went every Saturday. Soon on Sundays as well. I would
bring in goods from the town to save Angela the trip. Her mother
was no trouble – after mine she seemed a very sweet old lady,
very happy to talk endlessly about her life in that area sixty and
seventy years before, and then call on recollections of her
grandfather. I have always liked to hear people talking about
their own past and she had a crystal memory. It was no hardship.

She pretended to be a little put out when I proposed to Angela
– "I thought you were my young man," she said – but when I
said I would move into the farm she cheered up enormously.
Angela was not so keen but there was little alternative. The old
lady would not move and she could not be left alone.

The wedding was simple enough. Two aunts of mine on my
father's side made the journey. Angela's brother came with his
family. The bank and the tennis club made a respectable showing.
We went to Cornwall for our honeymoon. Angela got rather
badly sunburnt.

We lived on the farm for almost five years. I calculate that
you were born just as we left it and moved into the town.
Angela's mother died ('reluctantly' was Angela's curious word)
after a long and peaceful last phase during which her face became
translucently pure. I would go up to gaze at it sometimes when
she was asleep. Quite extraordinarily thin and clear, the tender
blue veins a visible network. The hair white and abundant to the
end.

I would have enjoyed staying on at the farm. I liked pottering
about the yard and the fields during the weekends pretending
to be a farmer. I liked being out of the town – away from the
customers. Especially as it seemed they would be my customers
for a long time now. A better job had come up in Mother's last
months but of course I could not take it.

However, Angela was firm. She had lived on the farm long

enough. She wanted to be in the town where there was "always something going on".

I can't tell you how happy I was in the first few years [she wrote]. I just can't express it. I seemed to fit into your skin. Now I try to think of things that came between us and the first was the money. Farmland had gone up in the Sixties and when everything was realised and divided I was left with a lot of heavy old furniture (which you would not let me throw out) and more than £82,000. That was a great deal of money in those days and we were both a bit flabbergasted. The first thing we decided to do was not tell anybody and although it was difficult – the amount had been published in the *Cumberland News* (I always think it is such an intrusion – why are they allowed to do it?) we studiously ignored enquiries however tactfully put. We bought this house which is nice but no palace; you refused to get a bigger car until you could afford one yourself. I wanted to do something mad like fly to Venice or – best of all – go on safari. You thought it would be too showy. Secretly I wanted to take some of the money and go to one of those clinics where the stars get their noses changed and their faces lifted and their bosoms straightened out and get them to scrape off my freckles but I did not come within a million miles of having the nerve to let on.

You locked the money away and it's been locked away ever since. I know that you've invested it very wisely because you have showed me every scrap of paper involved. It's swollen up to a terrible pile. I remember being stunned when it reached half a million. But we do nothing with it! It just sits there. I began to feel worried about it early on. I used to wish it had been in gangster pound notes in a suitcase and then I could have burnt it or thrown it away. I'm sure that would have been better. I could feel it festering there sometimes. It came between us – no doubt about that. Was it because it could make it seem that you had married me for money and your nature balked at that? I suppose it was; and I respect you for that.

Even June's wedding had to come out of your pocket.

She too came between us, didn't she? At first I thought that she completed everything. She was a very docile little thing. A smiling child. Never any trouble. Of course you fell head over heels for her like all fathers for their daughters. But the harder you tried, the more she flinched away. I would watch it and not be able to fathom it. Some sort of throwback gene in her nature made her cold. Rather like my mother had been to me, she was to you. I could see how difficult it was for you to tolerate it but I couldn't help. Her attitude did not get to me like it did to you. We tried for more children but it was not to be.

You worked so hard with June. Taking her everywhere. Playing with her. Being the life and soul of the birthday party, the Christmas party, the school party, the Sunday School outing, the Brownies' Annual Social, the Anglican Young People's Association walk – but it all slid over her. Not that she was mean to you: I think she was unaware of the impact she was having at first and then, in her early teens, it rather amused her and it was then that you went off her. You were never less than kind and loving but I could tell you had gone off her. Something in you had been worn down, worn down and then snubbed, and you turned away from it. I couldn't help you then; I should have done.

It was then that you started to bother on with your Lake District and the writing business and I was glad because you needed an outlet. You were bank manager by then and in Rotary and the Masons and for a while a church warden but your heart was in none of it. This new hobby seemed to give you a focus.

When you began to stay away at weekends I worried because I remembered the previous weekends and my suspicions at the time. But I beat them down. If you let them grow they can choke you. I had not been well for some time – a virus the doctor called it but no cure

he suggested seemed to do the trick. I was full of a
terrible lassitude. I tried to snap out of it as you know
and I've never been afraid of hard work. But I would
be OK for a day or two and then I'd sink back into it,
into an exhaustion that was really frustrating because I
could not seem to beat it.

I was in this state one Sunday some time ago,
standing at the window, waiting for you. June had gone
off to Australia by then and the house felt glum and
empty despite all that oak furniture which you would never
let me throw out. I was probably feeling sorry for myself
– a bad habit I tried to avoid. But illness is boring:
after the interest of finding out what you might have,
the limitations can get you down. And nobody really
likes being shackled to a sick person – not even you,
even you. I saw the car come and I stepped back. You
got out and something happy must have been on your
mind because you were smiling, looking years younger,
fresh and springing – you looked just as you did when
you walked into the bank on that first day and I went
head over heels. I could have cried to see you so full of
yourself, so handsome, so alive.

Then you turned to the house – to me, although you
could not see me – and your expression changed
completely. As if a mask had been ripped off. You looked
resigned, weary, even stooped a fraction, older; you
looked bored.

I had lost you.

I had lost you months, maybe years, before but I did
not let myself acknowledge it until that Sunday afternoon.
You called up with that regular cheerfulness and I called
back. You asked me if I wanted a cup of tea and I said
yes. You said you would bring it up and you did and the
man who entered my bedroom was lost to me.

Had my plainness finally oppressed you? My
obstinate illness worn you away? Or was it just in the
nature of these things? After all it is asking a lot for two
people to meet and marry at one age and still to be as
keen on each other twenty or thirty years on. It cannot

be in everybody's nature. You notice that as soon as
people get the money or the freedom to chop and change
a bit they very often take advantage. I've never blamed
them. In some ways I have always had a sneaking regard
for the likes of Elizabeth Taylor and her seven husbands.

So I could not blame you. And when I looked at myself
in the mirror! I'm sixty now, but on that Sunday afternoon
I was already looking sixty. I had gone the way of my
father, a big-bottomed heavy-limbed man and I had
been born too early for these diets and slimming. I had
let myself go. It never occurred to me that what I felt
for you needed words or any other proof. It was so deep
and right: it was everything I had. You are the only
person who has ever mattered to me – even more than
June after her first few years and even then . . . My
life has been made by knowing you. There is nothing
else.

To know that I had lost you was unbearable.

I took the coward's way. Asking for your pity I guess.
I became more bed-bound with my radio and my library
books, the cigarettes and the nips of whisky. I occupied
myself with world affairs and novels. There is scarcely
one important news bulletin that I miss and I am addicted
to all those discussion programmes. I know about
China and Russia, about the drug trade in Colombia and
the war in Ethiopia, about Sri Lanka and the Contras in
Nicaragua, and the Common Market; equally from
novels I know about the rise and fall of love affairs. I know
that people seem much more outspoken now – if novels
are anything to go by – and much less inhibited about
everything. I envy that. I've missed that. I've never
been modern. And now these damned pains which I know
Geoffrey thinks are serious. It took some perseverance
to make him postpone the X-ray until tomorrow but I
wanted a chance to talk to you. As it happens you have
been away a lot. Anyway – I've never been able to tell
you what I feel. Hence this letter.

What it says is very simple really. It says I am old
before my time – sixty can be young for some these days:

not for me. I feel old and I look old and there you are.
Not much fun for you. None at all.

So if you want to have another go – I won't stand in
your way. You've been very very good to me and
that's all I will remember. I could not bear it if I weighted
you down now and stopped you enjoying some
happiness. I wish it could be with me but that is not the
case. So I don't want to spoil it for you. That's all I'm
saying, darling. I love you very much. I wish I had said
that before. I wish I had said it even half the times I
thought it. You have given me so much and whatever
you do my love for you will be unimpaired.

Be free. Let me give you something for a change.
That would bring me great pleasure, truly. And don't
fret. You've been the love of my life.

I went upstairs to talk to her and hug her but she was too deeply
asleep to disturb, snoring slightly, but I had long ago trained
myself to tolerate that. She looked old, and worn; but there was
still that sweetness and innocence I had once loved so much. I
knew that I could never leave her. She needed to be taken care
of.

SIXTEEN

Your letter came on the Wednesday morning, second post. It was addressed with tact – a plain envelope, my name typed. It could have been any one of several notifications I still received. To my surprise I did not rip it open or fall on it with relief: the very sight of it – for though it was disguised to the world, I knew it was yours – made me feel even more desperate. I was convinced that now I would certainly lose you. I was tired to death.

The tiredness was not just a fatigue in the mind but also in the limbs, in the chest, a turgidness in the blood, like the early stages of a severe bout of flu, I suppose, if one is straightforward about it, but without the excuse of a virus.

I had driven Angela to hospital on Monday and they had kept her in. I came back, packed a case, and returned to stay with her for the afternoon and early evening. They were very relaxed about visiting hours. She dozed for most of the time and I tried to read but as often as not my attention would wander. It would be flattering to report that my thoughts turned to you: my thoughts turned because of you no doubt, but also because of Angela. There was quite simply a numbed sense of impasse. I had been hurtling in a certain direction and now the way was blocked. I could not see beyond the obstacle. The course I had was to be patient. The prospect of unremitting patience over an unspecified time was the spiritual virus.

And of course – but how I betray myself by introducing it so late – *of course*, I wrote – Angela's illness was not only an obstacle, it was grief. Already in two days it had moved her towards the centre of my concerns. I am trying to be honest – although is honesty sometimes so very important? What would Angela have gained from my honesty if I had said – "Look. I love someone else. There is no point in pretending. I am an honest man. I will do my marital duty – fetch and carry, observe all visiting hours – but I have to tell you that my heart is not in it and nor is it with you." Hypocrisy has its place. And it was much more complicated than that – the toytown battles between honesty and hypocrisy soon merged into the adult confusion of emotional relativity.

For Angela's illness, her stoicism – she hid the pain but the surgeon told me that it must be considerable – her sweetness, that unselfish lovingness, reactivated early feelings of my own. Let me try to be as accurate as possible. She was not nor has she ever been a cipher. She did not use unselfishness as a tactic in the sense of using surrender to prevent hurt. There was nothing simpering or feeble about her, nor was she passive. She had, as her letter shows you, a capacity for constant unimpaired affection which included the idea that I must not be shackled. I had always known that. Although I do not make a song and dance about it, that matters a great deal to me. Our recognition of each other's essential freedom was part of our marriage – in our own under-standing way – and it had kept me faithful to her for years until you appeared like a comet to destroy all my careful arrangements with the universe of the affections.

Perhaps unsurprisingly then, in the space of two days concern and sympathy grew to rediscovery of love and gratitude. Yet I knew that true as those feelings were, they were in a different category from the feelings I had and have for you. They were 'finer' perhaps, by society's standards, 'better' moralists would certainly say – they may be right. But should I recognise their rules when the whole point of my feelings for you is that the rules were broken? Nevertheless if meeting you was volcanic, meeting Angela's illness was at first like the volcano being capped. Still there, still throbbing, firing; but capped. Just when I needed all my forces to win you back – I was drawn away.

The cancer was well developed but before they rushed to operate they wanted to do a number of tests. Her weakness made that in itself difficult. She ought to have complained much earlier. I did not challenge her on this, fearing perhaps that the answer might further condemn my behaviour. As it was I felt the pressure of guilt like thumb pressure under the ears. So often the illness of someone close to you makes you reproach yourself. Partly for the relief – however fleeting – that it is not you. And when you have guilt already waiting for you like an assassin in an alley, then its release can be convulsive. As it was with me. Her illness triggered the guilt. My tiredness was the tiredness of one being pounded by remorse: and yet I still loved you as much, even then. Another planet had reappeared, that was all: not displacing yours. But had I lost you?

Your letter was short and dry – do you remember? Could we meet soon, you had something to say: followed by a list of where you would be at different times. The list was rather touching – was the list my influence? 5.30 – in the office ready to leave; 7.30 – Thursday/Friday usual pub; Saturday – free all day – up street 10 – 12 to make it easy, either Spotted Cow Snack Bar or waiting about shops. Clearly you had not heard of Angela's hospitalisation.

Nor had you read her letter. It was important for me to remember that. To remember exactly how we had parted. On 'fighting terms', in a phrase: our first ever dispute. In your head, though, must have been the clear shock of my Hazlitt inspired accusations. My thoughts were soaked in Angela: her letter, the cancer, the press of memory, the drain of guilt. I was a different man. Perhaps you interpreted my subdued state as evidence of an unspoken apology. You did not know that she was ill.

You looked younger than ever. The washed-out tight jeans, the red shoes, a white blouse – more like a shirt – a pullover slung around your neck for the colder late evening; a smile so fresh it all but brought tears to my eyes. I was *that* weak. You got in the car and ordered me to take you to the seaside town.

You acted as if I had done nothing wrong and your chatter easily filled out the short drive. For the first time I felt that I was being unfaithful to Angela. Believe that or not but as you must know by now these confessions try to tell the whole truth. At long last I felt unfaithful to a wife I had cheated for months and with no great care for appearances.

You directed me half a mile or so away from the small town's centre, north along the Solway coast past a ribbon development of what were chiefly retirement bungalows. I had not thought to walk up there when I had come to spy on you.

"I believe you," I said, before you said a word.

"I'd like you to meet her anyway."

"I'd rather believe you."

"She's great. She'll be glad to see a new face. She's very cut off."

I did not want to meet your 'sister'. I was too troubled to take her on.

"Look . . . I'm sorry I was so untrusting."

"We all have bad times. I should have told you the truth from the start. My fault, partly anyway."

"Was it always your sister you went to see?"

I had stopped the car a few yards off the road beside some tall gaunt pines. Between the railings of the trunks we saw the fretting Solway Firth.

"Why don't you come and see her?" Your voice was small and frightened. I wanted to touch your hair, cover your face with my hand. Instead the voice of hateful destructive jealousy broke out again – as if NOTHING had happened between our last meeting and this one.

"What about the weekdays? When you avoided me. It couldn't always have been your sister."

"I said I would be bringing her a surprise," you said. "Please come. It's just down there, second on the right."

"Why don't you tell me about the weekdays?"

"There's nothing to say."

"That man – a young man – I saw you talking with in the pub – the first time I came in the pub – talking to very closely . . . ?"

"Which man?"

"A dark suit, very wavy black hair, thick, all going back, a very white face."

"I can't remember. I can't remember. I'm sorry. I can't."

"And that letter –"

"Please."

"All you have –"

"Please – please don't. I wish to God I'd never written it."

"Why?"

"It lets you know how dirty I am."

"What *do* you mean?"

"Spoiled." You spoke very sadly. "Forever spoiled. You needn't have known that."

"I was moved, I was very moved by your letter."

"But now you don't believe a word of it."

"I do. I just want you –"

"To prove it? How can I prove it? My mother and Joe will say nothing about it even if the thumbscrews are on them. We never admit to that sort of thing in our family. So how do I prove it?"

"I believe you."

"But you don't. I can tell that you don't."

"I do now."

"I shouldn't have sent it."

"But what you said about your feelings for me, in the letter . . ."

"I meant them." You spoke the next sentences so matter-of-factly that it took days for the force of them to register. "You have no idea how much I love you. You *are* my life."

"So why did you avoid me?"

"All right." You turned to face me and stared without blinking. I remember my discomfort: not being able to look away; not being able to look. "I was worried about your wife. You've scarcely talked about her but from what I've heard she's a very nice decent person and I've tried not to think about her. You've hardly mentioned her and I've never pressed you. My excuse has always been – he'll bring it up when he's good and ready. But that's no good really. I'm just as responsible as you are. I was behaving like your little girl and – don't deny it – sometimes you like that. But we were seeing far too much of each other in the town and *being seen* far too much. Especially at lunchtime or you always turning up on the dot at 5.30. You can get away with it for a while with saying I'm working for you and you're taking me up. A lot of people are prepared to believe that. Especially of somebody like you – a bank manager and the articles in the papers. Besides – what would you see in a slut from the Kennedy clan? But after a little while tongues will start to wag. I wanted to delay that if I could. On the few occasions you *have* talked about your wife you've been very warm about her, you've been more than just loyal. I've been jealous of her but funnily enough I'd like to meet her. Never can though. Not now . . . Anyway, that was the reason for cutting down on the meetings."

Your intuition had never been more evident, more precisely targeted.

I sat for a long time in silence. Let me say again that you had no idea about the letter Angela had just written or about her admission into the hospital. My mood of guilt, shame, sorrow must have moved you because you discarded your own legitimate grievance and reached out – literally, putting your hand in mine – to help. There was no way out of it.

"The truth is," I said, finally, "that Angela is in hospital. I took her there on Monday and they kept her in. She has cancer. They think it might be very bad."

Those four sentences took the heart out of me. I had mumbled the whole story out at a windscreen beginning to speckle with drizzle which came with the dusk. No cars on the coast road on such an unattractive end of season night. One or two people walking their dogs, but in the distance, beyond the pines. You did not let go of my hand.

"Well then," you said, shaking my hand, as if to wake me gently. "That's it."

"Is it?"

"We can't see each other while she's ill."

"Why not?"

"It would be terrible."

"What will you do?" I asked.

"Wait for you."

"Shall we see each other?"

"We can't, can we? Not when she's in hospital. Not when she's so ill."

"So what are you saying?"

"I'll wait for you."

"Until –"

"Doesn't matter." You actually put your index finger to my lips. "Doesn't matter."

"So this is it?"

"Yes."

"How can you be so calm about it?"

"I don't feel calm. I don't want to feel anything at the moment."

"Are you quite pleased to be getting rid of me?" What made me say that? You were strong enough to ignore me but when I persisted – and persisted – you opened the door and you were out of the car and away before I could convert my suspicion and lunatic jealousy into shame and the will to catch you.

Second turning on the right you had said. That is where I went and found an avenue of pastel-coloured bungalows – most of them very small indeed – but no sight of you.

I could have knocked on every door but instead I walked up and down looking in vain for signs of a disabled person – a wider than usual door, ramps where steps would have been – and peering through windows hoping for a glimpse of you. I saw televisions and attentive bodies watching across fitted carpets. No ramps. No evidence.

My feelings of hopelessness – on all fronts – is best left undocumented. Finally I drove away. I never did ask you how you got back.

The next day was spent at the hospital. I was telephoned in the morning and was told that Angela was going in for major surgery. I went down immediately, in sufficient time to talk a little before the anaesthetic. She was in the operating-theatre for over two hours and as I was told she could wake up any time after six or seven hours I went straight home to be beside a phone. June had to be contacted although I emphasised that she need not come over yet. The surgeon told me that he thought he had checked the spread of it.

Your note was there.

You must be very very upset so don't make it worse for
yourself by worrying about last night. That was trivial by
comparison. Sorry I ran away. Behaved like a wimp. I
do hope everything works out – for your wife. As for us
– I'll wait for you. I don't expect to see you – until you
think it's the right time. I'll wait. Love, Bernadette.
XXX

Like Angela, you had given me what was apparently an easy way out. Like Angela you knew – you must have known – that nothing else could tie me in so securely.

There is injustice in that statement but truth enough to say that you made it hard by making it easy. But why should it be easy? I was a middle-aged and normal man having an affair with a teenaged girl (although teenager never seemed to fit you) and my wife was discovered to be seriously ill. By all my own standards I should have been roasting in a purgatory of my own making. No matter the statistics on divorce – most of which I am sure come after agonising, desolate and terrible unrecorded traumas, the largely hidden costs and battles of late twentieth-century domestic life – no matter that 'attitudes' are said to have 'relaxed' about promiscuity, *I* disapproved of myself very strongly. Your presence, our passion had burned that disapproval to a frazzle. But like my affection for Angela, it rose to the surface, commanded into activity by her illness.

I replied to your note and arranged a date but you were firm. Not until the circumstances were more favourable, you said. I found that I agreed with you and I was relieved. For in that short time, her illness had taken me over. Severe illness colonises those around it. Even the cat became too much of a distraction and I gave her away, not without remembering the first time she had occupied your chair.

Angela was so obviously cheered up by my visits that there was no need for the surgeon and staff to lay it on about how much it helped. Because of the severity of her surgery they had put her in a private room. Should there be another emergency, they would have to put her back in a general ward, they said. This was fair enough. But she derived great comfort from being on her own. I know others of the opposite disposition. I knew Angela's preference and I was determined that if necessary I would pay for a private room – I was told that payment could secure it without any trouble. So the money could finally help her.

She was very weak but she made more efforts than she had made for many years. The complaint or virus or psychosomatic disturbance which had kept her to her bed over the last few years had reinforced her shyness and fed her tentative nature: she had been very little inclined to talk. Now conversation seemed to be her chief nourishment.

There was something marvellous in it. I have observed it

three times now – with my own mother, with Angela's mother, and with Angela herself. Close companionship and constant nursing make a degree of difference. It is as if the feeding of the mind, the fortifying of the spirit through daily and intense contact, can stem – at least for a while – the ravages on the body. It is another spell.

My mother wanted to talk about my day. Nothing else would satisfy her. Perhaps that is how I got into the habit of detailed memory. The only thing for it was to begin by saying whom I had met as I walked down the street to the bank; who was before me and after me at the bank; when I served my first customer in the bank and who that customer was. As she was a stranger to the town the description of the customers was initially a rather laborious business. She had nothing to cling on to. Nobody came up who was related to her or with whom she had been to school; nor could she construct this world from people she saw in the street, so rarely did she go out. It must have been like listening to the radio. Because of her isolation and her utter trustworthiness I broke the fundamental rule of banking now and then and, to spice up a story or help define a character, would tell her of some financial transaction. She liked that. All very thrifty people are fascinated by money and for thrift my mother wore the crown. No wonder I found the work at the bank so easy. Some part of every evening was spent in revising it, as if I were preparing for an exam. Soon she got the hang of the 'regulars' and would pick out certain characters, things which irritated or pleased her – almost always to their detriment. She had exacting standards and rigid principles.

If this seems rather a sad tale, with me in thrall to an old dragon, I must assure you it was not so. You have to go a long way down the line of human misery before you encounter circumstances from which no good at all can be rescued and there was much satisfaction for me – of a slow and domestic kind – in these daily monologues and quizzings. They did not have to be protracted. It was restful and, after the turbulent uncertainties of a drunken father's faithless rule, it was welcome. Besides, I began to embroider 'my' characters and their stories: once or twice, to relieve the insistent pulse of the daily ordinary,

I would even invent something. I was both flattered and nervous to find these little flights of invention very often relished above all else. Further elaboration would be needed as the lie fed on itself and her unrelenting questioning spared nothing. It became quite difficult to remember what was truth and what was lies and to help me out – or later to prevent her from catching me out – I began to keep a record, a 'journal' I rather grandly called it. The principal purpose of this was to set down what I had made up so that I did not trip myself up in succeeding chapters. But other matters began to find their home in the little silent notepads and the habit of jotting began. When Mother died that habit was a balm to me. I could immerse myself in the writing for an hour or so and come out of it at least soothed, often refreshed. You see, I loved her.

Angela's mother was dominated by her childhood which in old age she saw as pretty and protected as one of those small Tudor, walled rose gardens. Nothing was there which was not magical. The pony and trap which had taken her to school. The smocks the girls wore to keep off the chalk. The *real* slate they wrote on. The gentle teachers and friendly pupils. The way her father dressed his show horses, brushing the mane, glossing the coat, plaiting the tail with flowers, polishing the hooves. The servant-girl helping her mother to bake and so much being taken in from the fields and hedgerows to make such 'tasty' meals then: the taste all gone today. Angela's mother was a chronicler of her own life which had intrigued her – up to the age of about sixteen: after that there were leaps and sudden pools of interest. But the steady narrative was in those years just before and after the turn of the century when golden harvests lit up the fields, when all men carried knives to cut their tobacco or for whittling at a piece of wood, or for the general use which would be met with in a day's work – and all the women were ferocious bakers and makers-do on very little but yet providers on an epic scale. When a mouth organ and a few brave voices would be the evening's entertainment and a day out at a fair could contain more adventure than a package fortnight on the coast of Spain.

Angela had taken refuge in the news of the day. Her radio discussions and her one serious, one popular newspaper (two

of the qualities on Sunday and one 'pop', as I sometimes said,
to wash them down); her regular lists to the library for the latest
biography or essay on our times and a certain natural seriousness
had given her many years of quiet absorption. I remembered
then (too late) how often in the past she had tried to throw out
a line, hoping I would grab it and haul alongside a conversation
on the Environment or Nuclear Weapons or Was There A
Solution to Northern Ireland? or the Middle East or South Africa
– but so often my engagement had failed to come up to scratch.
She was especially taken by the progress of the Greens – the
first time for years, she said, she had personally been interested
in politics. Whatever I said, she would encourage me by praise,
hoping for a 'real' discussion such as those we had enjoyed in
the early days when her rather radical views and my restrained
politic (bank policy) conservatism led to some lively clashes of
opinion. But my opinion was that the world was too full of
information and cynicism, overloaded with alternatives, under-
provided with solutions, the whole thing beggared by politicians
who, even the best of them, I thought, sadly, were more
interested in getting and holding power than in identifying and
solving real problems. That was my rationale. The truth was
that during those years I was not sufficiently interested in
Angela.

Now once more I was. Necessity can be the mother of
affection. Thrown together we had to survive together and I
took several newspapers down. The *Independent* and *Guardian*
were our weekdays with the *Telegraph* and *Times* on Saturday
and on Sunday the *Observer* and the *Sunday Times*. *Mails*
figured regularly with a dash of *Expresses* and the occasional
glittering monthly.

The nurses soon labelled her room 'Newspaper Library' and
she was indeed curiously loath to have any of the papers thrown
away until she had, as she said, 'given them a chance'. Her
tiredness meant that I had to read the stories aloud most of the
time which made me appreciate how well so many of the stories
were written and, after a while, how gripping a daily addiction
to the news could become. The long progress of a strike, the
surprise of a natural catastrophe, the running commentary on
the ups and downs of the parties, an oil slick, bombardments

and continual casualties in war games, which seemed almost to have been marked out as the places in which the world was allowed to behave at its worst, the saga of drugs in the American cities and the drug barons of Colombia (a story which, as with anything on the Mafia, greatly intrigued Angela), Gorbachev's fight to revolutionise Russia and the opening up of the Eastern bloc . . . there was no end to it. It had suspense and variety and excitement of an order which had never entranced me as much in adventure stories or action films. Angela was right. The world out there was a gripping story and we were in it and we could read about it and it was both true and fantastical. She had a vivid sense of that, which grew more intense as the condition worsened.

Sometimes I would instigate – suddenly prompted by a warm recollection – a story of our early days together on the farm or at the tennis club but, though patient enough, she was inclined to give it short shrift. There was a world out there written to be read and she wanted to know about it. She lusted for the present.

After three weeks she was moved back home – downstairs – my study was transformed into her bedroom despite her protests. It was then that I hoped to see you again when I walked downtown to do the shopping (a day nurse would sit in for me). Never a glimpse.

While I was disappointed I was also impressed. The two of us were working together for someone else. What better way to strengthen our mutual regard and feelings? I missed you – very much. But you had come out of the blue, breaking the chastity of many years, and so my habit was much more developed towards doing without than doing with. I could rationalise it like that. But the earlier description was better. The volcano had been (temporarily) capped. I was occupied with my dying wife.

There could be no doubt now. Just over a month at home and she was back in the hospital. It had broken out again and again she had a major operation and again we had the small private room (this time paying) and this time I did all the reading of the newspapers. Or we would sit and listen to programmes on Radio Four or, sometimes, music on Radio Three. It is surprising how often an unplanned piece of music can seem to describe and resolve an entire mood: as if there is a hidden coincidence in the occurrence of things, a serendipity for those – like Angela – who call out for it.

For her innocence and purity of heart shone through. Like white rays coming through clouds in a Lakeland sky. All the doctors and the nurses remarked on it. The friends who came to see her said the same. An ethereal serenity possessed her and as if the age of miracles had not passed, her freckles gradually, slowly, began to disappear. It left her face as white as fresh linen. I showed her in the mirror and she was not coy. "Better late . . ." she said, and smiled so happily.

We became interested in the medical reports in the newspapers but found them lacking in detail. Mr Elliott, the senior surgeon, supplied us with some professional magazines and what you might consider morbid we found to be compelling: the many forms and routes and theories on cancer. I think it helped Angela because she had to face drastic treatments in curing her and knowing the whys and the wherefores was some comfort. There were times when the jolts of cure threatened her – in my observation – more than the cancer itself.

Why drag it out? It did drag out, for several more months, but they were months of the same. Just that the graph of decline set in and was unyielding. Every week a visible ink line nearer death. Angela did not like to talk about it. She did not rage at it but nor did she acquiesce in it through fatigue or not wanting to bother anyone any more. With her limited resources she got on with as much of life as she could encompass. I did – quite early on – suggest that we raid what was now her quite formidable accumulation of wealth so that she could do the things she had only dreamed of: but no. No blame to me. No sad-eyed "If only you had suggested that in the early days . . ." Just "No thanks" and on to the next thing. The eagerness of her mind, her determination to keep up with the history of the world we lived in, not only its news but its discoveries and its ideas and opinions, that was ever more touching the weaker she became.

There came a time when I signalled for June to come over. She had left for Australia as reedy and rather angular as I am. She came back as plump as Angela had once been and full to the

brim with the open affection so lacking in her as a girl. She was
marvellous at doing all the sorting out of Angela's things –
labelling this pile to go to an old people's home, that to Oxfam
. . . But I rush ahead of myself. I go before my horse to market
as Angela's mother used to say.

I did not see her die. I had left an hour earlier. But June had
taken over from me and so she did not die alone.

SEVENTEEN

June left about a fortnight later after what I think was a sincere effort to take me with her. It was out of the question but I was very touched by her insistence and during that final drive down to Heathrow I was the closest I had ever been to her. I promised her I would come out to Australia sooner or later and we parted affectionately. Angela had left her half the money which meant that she returned home an unexpectedly wealthy woman. The other half and the house and, of course, my own savings stayed with me. These, together with the pension, gave me more than enough not only for a comfortable but for an adventurous life.

I cannot explain to you why it took me another three weeks to make a move to see you. I have thought about it hard and often, but it eludes me. Of course I needed a time to mourn. But why had I put a block on my feelings for you not only during those three weeks but throughout Angela's illness? Guilt could explain a lot, I suppose, but it gets so complicated. For why did I not feel guilty about neglecting you? Was I so very sure of you?

Maybe this is desperation. I feared that if I let you into my life and into my mind then I would walk away from Angela and what would that do but harm? We could wait. Sometimes I think it was the pressure of not seeing you throughout her illness which led me to that terrible numbness and silence in the weeks after her death. The shock of her death and the shock of delivery – we could have a life – clashed and crushed me. But I still cannot understand it, still less excuse it – though sometimes I feel that I must if I am to have any hope of reaching you again. So the anxiety worries on and on. And, crazily, I thought that Angela had died to make it easier for me. I cannot explain how appalled I felt by the insistence of that contaminating thought.

Of course I was tired – over the last few months and especially over the last weeks the strain had been relentless: at times I was possessed of the rather insane, unremitting thought that it was the intensity of my concentration on her and nothing else which kept her alive. Empathy turned to hypnosis and – though I am fearful to tell you this – love. The love which I have for you is unique and beyond my understanding. The love I grew to have for Angela was different in all particulars but common in one basic characteristic: it obsessed me. It obsessed me that I be there to try to will her through another day.

But it was not only the tiredness. I missed her. I missed those acres of time increasingly by the radio, both of us listening intently to talk or to music as if we were in some resistance movement waiting for a code to be smuggled through on the air-waves. I missed her gallantry and curiosity. I wanted a time to mourn. Yes, Angela's death could in some twisted way have seemed convenient for us: in fact it seemed to create a chasm between us. As long as she was alive – so were we. Would her death finish us off?

Forgive me but I never told her about us. This was not to negate us or in any way diminish us but what would have been the point? I wanted to boast of you. In my more extravagant moments I wanted to bring you along and introduce you to Angela. Angela, this is Bernadette. Bernadette, this is Angela. You'll be so good for each other.

Or was I frightened of what I would discover? So pleased with myself at being capable of scaling cliffs of passion and sexual fulfilment unknown, I feared it might all have been a fluke, unrepeatable. I confess there was a little of that. And, however much I rationalise it, there was also the *weird* triumph we had pulled off: after months of dashing around the Lake District tearing off each other's clothes, we were, or rather I was, now content to appear as a distant, restrained figure. Above all we had kept our word. *We* had done the right thing and helped Angela. But had the obsession gone, worn itself out or found that compared with the steady force of deep affection it had to race away like a vampire faced by a crucifix? Moreover, not only how had *I* managed – how had *you*? For you – in that letter – had confessed to a terrible preoccupation with me and often enough I had felt the truth and force of it. How had you directed it while we were so long apart? Or how had you controlled it? *Had* you?

Yet the edge of my suspicion had gone. The poison which had passed into me from that book – and, as I know, although you gamely concealed it for Angela's benefit, deeply affected you as well – was only a thing of regrets. The time with Angela and the death of Angela had put that in its place. It was still capable of suppurating. I would not rule it out, but only perhaps when the passion was physically resumed. The jealousy could be part of the eroticism, although I hoped not. In any case there were calm waters at that moment, I thought. How stoic you had been was what I convinced myself: not one letter or phone call for months. How restrained – both of us, how true to our word.

But the time had come at last to seek you out and reclaim you. I had put my house on the market and received an offer which was thirty-four times (3,400%) more than I had paid for it. Yet more money. I had begun to think in terms of asking you to leave your job and come on a grand tour for three months, for six months, for a year: first through Britain and then over Europe; and beyond if the wind blew us there. It was as if, that spring Wednesday afternoon, I had completed something in myself. I went to the cemetery (Angela had insisted that she did not want to be cremated) and from there to my old post outside Christopher's office, treading in the footsteps of my past.

You failed to show up. Nor were you in the pub and I decided to come down later.

The pub was less than half full, even at nine o'clock. The landlady looked at me with little variation of her usual disdain: I had not seen her for months and was puzzled at first until I remembered her never-articulated enmity. Joe was there; not pleased to see me although he was polite enough to fake a certain cheeriness.

"Have a drink," I offered.

"Right." He sank what was almost a full pint, concluding the trick by slamming it down in front of me.

I had a scotch. I had used it quite sparingly though, it has to be admitted, regularly over the months. Joe was politely grateful for the drink but unforthcoming: not about *you*; about everything. Usually we would manage a very sociable conversation or 'crack' as he called it. As often as not he would tell me local stories, episodes from a semi-criminal life in the outdoors. My return to him was either some titbit of local lore – the location of old mine shafts, the feasibility of discovering marketable quantities of silver or gold in the rivers – or, more effectively, I explained some manoeuvrings on the Stock Market and the take-over business, whose millions and billions could mesmerise Joe for some time.

Nothing got under way that night. Eventually I asked if you might be dropping in and he said "Very unlikely." No more. At that stage, still coming out of shock and numbness, I did not fully register the danger in his tone.

I looked out for you the next day at lunch and again there was no sign. Perhaps you had gone on your holidays. That was a perfectly adequate explanation and one would have thought it would do, especially after my very successful hibernation of feelings. But mid-way through the afternoon my nerve went and I phoned your office.

I was told you had left your job, two or three months ago.

Where were you now?

The girl did not know.

I asked to be put through to Christopher.

"Why did she leave?"

Christopher's pipe sucked in the pause even more dramatically and then he said:

"You mean you really didn't know."

"Of course not. Don't you realise –?"

"Sorry. Sorry. Sorry, old chap." He had been to the funeral and behaved impeccably. He appeared not to be put out that the will was in the hands of a solicitor in Carlisle.

"Was she falling down on the job?"

"No. Very few complaints."

"Just wanted a change?"

"Yes." Again the pause. "Look. Sure you don't know?" I did then. A fraction before he confirmed what swirled through me, engulfing my mind with a force and a dizziness I could not fully comprehend but somewhere in there was a great joy. "They *said* she was pregnant," he said.

With my child! My child! Our child – of course. *Ours!*

"Or that was the rumour," he continued, quickly.

"Where is she now?"

"The reason the rumour withered on the vine is because of the speed of her departure. Out of my office, out of the town and off the map as far as I can tell. Of course I have nothing to go on but office gossip. On the other hand, the others were very fond of her." There was ill-disguised surprise in that last sentence.

"You have no idea?"

"None. I would certainly tell you if I had."

"And the girls in the office?"

"None either. As a matter of fact they were just discussing her yesterday. Truth to relate – this was after seeing you hanging about outside. Nobody here has a clue."

I drove down to your house, as you must know, and met hostility.

"How do we know where she is?" Your mother's aggression was as thick as the cigarette smoke which coughed from her lips. I had caught her in curlers and slippers which might have added to the antagonism. Her appearance was markedly out of kilter with the lavish, colourful but brightly cared for furnishings of the room: it was like the inside of an old-fashioned Romany caravan. "You're the one who should know."

"I haven't heard from her for months."

"Oh no?"

"No. And I haven't been in contact with her for months."

"Why not?"

I explained about Angela – briefly, not wanting Angela to sound like an excuse.

"Well, I'm very sorry to hear it. But you had an obligation to my lassie too and she's gone. Vamoosed."

"Have you looked – ?"

"Have we looked!" That was scorn.

"Where might she have gone?"

"You tell us, mister. You put all them fancy ideas in her head."

Was she pregnant? I wanted to ask. Was she pregnant? Why

was it so difficult to ask this of a woman younger than myself smoking strong cigarettes and wearing her curlers?

"Why did she go?"

"Come off it."

"Please. I don't know. I've come to find out. As I've explained –"

"Don't be stupid."

Maybe that stung.

"Was she pregnant?"

"And whose bloody fault was it if she bloody was?"

"Was she?"

There was a sulky pause.

"She wouldn't say. She admitted nothing. Obstinate. She should never have stayed on at that school. Turned her into somebody else. She lost herself."

"Was she very disturbed – did you notice that she was very disturbed before she left?"

"She could be very difficult at times."

I took a breath. Forgive me, Bernadette, but the vile suspicion rose up again and here was a chance to slay it.

"Was that because of the lodger who raped her some years ago?"

"Bugger off!"

'It would help me to know."

"Bugger off! Bugger off!" She stood up, her short stature and powerful bosom quite commanding in that small room. "And you can thank your lucky stars none of my lads is at home. Bugger off!"

"Mrs Kennedy. I want to find your daughter. I want to marry her. I need to know as much as possible."

"What lodger?"

"Bernadette told me."

"Oh she did, did she? What else did she say?"

"What else?"

"Who was to blame? That's what I want to know. Who was to blame? Not *her*. Not her royal bloody highness."

"So it *was* true."

Forgive me, Bernadette.

I think the phrase "I want to marry her" finally made it

through the smoke fumes and quite soon by one of those turns of fortune which I would guess characterise your mother, we were having tumblers of scotch while she cried over her loss of you.

Only later, only early the next morning, did I come to the conclusion that the Kennedy clan had closed ranks as usual. I became convinced that they *did* know where you were. But they and only they were to share that knowledge. I had to get it. Otherwise I could be looking all over the British Isles. I had, on the way back from your mother's, sought out the girl you had described as your best friend in the office and *she* did not know; and tracked down in the pubs the girls with whom you had gone to Blackpool and *they* did not know. The Kennedys did.

Would bribery do it? It could be the quickest way. I sought out Big Joe that night.

"Look," I said, when we had a corner free although I still felt obliged to talk out of the side of my mouth and look down at his dog as if I were addressing sweet nothings to the over-muscled monster, "I just want a lead. I know there may be reasons but I want to marry her for God's sake. Of course there will be problems and it may be difficult for you. That's why I know you'll have no hesitation in taking this." I palmed him thirty pounds in tenners and he neither looked at it nor registered the carefully folded little wad. "Where is she?"

"Beats me."

"You must know. Your mother knows."

"Does she?"

"I can sense that she does."

"She's said nothing to me, pal."

"There's more where that came from. Have a whisky." I went to the bar and did not look back – to give him the chance to count the money.

When I returned Joe had adopted a most thoughtful pose.

"Why're you so keen?"

"I want to marry her."

"Does she know?"

"How can I tell her until I find her?"

"True enough. Cheers." He drank off the whisky and looked

down at the clenched fist which had so skilfully absorbed the thirty pounds. He gave the appearance of one pondering.

"It'll take a bit of – you know, this and that."

"Enquiries?"

"This and that." Again he looked at the clenched fist and he may have shaken his head. I was prepared.

"I'll cover expenses," I said and palmed him another fifty pounds.

"Expenses," he nodded, as grateful for the word as for the money; well, almost.

"You'll let me know?"

"Count on it."

And so began a dance which lasted for a good fortnight, at the end of which I had parted with two hundred and thirty pounds and learnt all that Joe knew: nothing.

It was in that fortnight that I began to deteriorate. Having sold my house I deferred buying anything else (Would *you* like it? Would you approve?). The furniture was put in store and I looked for somewhere to rent. There was so little on the market that I settled for this. In some ways it was perfect for me. A slum, the only habitable cottage in a row about to be condemned, it matched the mood I was plunging towards, although for the first week or two I could feel superior to it. There was something hairshirt about it; something which undercut the comforts of your family's council house: it said 'Look what I am prepared to suffer'. The discomforts and plain inadequacies were a masochistic consolation. My mood was not merely being matched but anticipated. My sleeping was becoming irregular. Your name, your voice, your face hammered inside my brain. I began to long for you again and the desire tormented itself on revisiting a past which reinforced the barren present. I understand how longing can become a sickness.

When Joe finally admitted – or pretended to admit – that he knew nothing, that he had uncovered nothing and there was nothing to report, I was so frustrated – and drunk – that I did something most unusual for me and began to swear loudly. The landlady asked me to leave. I refused; her cold little eyes, the eyes of the pleasure-hating moralist, provoked my stubbornness and I would not go. She threatened to call the police. The public took a keen interest. Joe tried to intervene and see me off the premises. In my desperate and fuddled state I hit out at him, whereupon he clasped his arms about me, lifted me bodily from the floor and, amid some laughter, carried me not only out onto the street but round into the church square where he dropped me on a bench and told me to sober up. I hope I thanked him.

Worse, much worse, followed. As you know, I went back to the pub the next night, had the last-minute wit to apologise effusively to the landlady who – I was reliably informed – was all set to bar me, and I challenged your mother. That is to say I tried, first of all, to make her drunk. We drank glass for glass – her ghastly potion and my scotch – and in the end I was literally legless. I had never been legless before. I thought it was just a colourful expression. No. Once more Big Joe carried me out. He and Theresa and her boyfriend took me to my car and the boyfriend made a fair job of getting me down to my new home without completely wrecking the vehicle. Big Joe was very unimpressed by my new premises and said so.

Then I lay in wait for your mother in the mornings when she shopped.

By now, the alcohol, the desperation – where were you? Where was the child? – were melding into terror. I was in a labyrinth without exits. How could I find you and bring you back?

I went to see your doctor who said he knew nothing and even if he had known something could not have told me and recommended tranquillisers, saying that I was suffering from delayed shock over the death of Angela. He wrote out a prescription but I did not cash it in. Whisky would have to do.

I pursued Theresa – sure that she would know as you and she seemed closest in the family, but she turned on me with a mouthful of fishwife bile which I thought had gone out of fashion: her point seemed to be that I was a dirty old man and but for me her darling sister would not be on the Missing Persons List which is what the situation amounted to, she said.

Though still convinced that the Kennedys were holding out, I went to the police and, after some difficulty, failed to get your picture onto a Missing Persons poster. Your family would not co-operate. No Kennedy, it seemed, had ever been a missing person. I thought of sending details off to one of the national

tabloid newspapers which specialise in this area, but Big Joe
promised that "The family will deny it". By then even his
patience was running thin. He refused expenses and his tone
was hostile.

Within a few weeks I managed to alienate all your family. My
reputation in the town began its descent to present proportions.
I found that my energy worked in curious ways: I could not find
the will to shave, for instance – why not? Nor did I want to
change clothes from one day to the next. While never having
been a fussy dresser, I had always been clean and neat – this
slippage was widely noted and together with the scarlet in the
cheeks, the whisky on the breath, turned me into a bogey-man,
a taunt for little boys.

I sat for hours making calculations. Would you have gone to
London? Very unlikely, too far from home. Into Scotland? No,
though I had heard you mention Glasgow as a place you'd like
to see. More likely were Manchester, Liverpool and Newcastle.
Newcastle was the handiest and in some ways the most natural
move: local people got up coach trips to shop in Newcastle.
But Manchester could seem big and somehow powerful – a place
where there would be plenty to do; and Liverpool, always a
possibility, always a chance in Liverpool.

What was I to do?

I rang up the central police stations in those cities. I then rang
up the maternity hospitals. I found out what hostels there were
for single persons and rang up those. Without the slightest
success. I thought of ringing up solicitors' offices to see if they
had taken you on as new staff. It took me more than a week. It
was not so bad. There was the constant anticipation and the
small disappointment of a negative answer was instantly rescued
by the hope with which I dialled the next call.

One day – blaming myself that I had not thought of this sooner
– I went to Graham's the barber, had my beard trimmed – it
was quicker than a shave – and hurried up to Christopher's to
try to put together your last hours in the town.

Christopher called in the girls and they gave me the date on
which they had last seen you and the time – that inevitable 5.30.
After that it would be over to the Kennedys. I knew they would
clam up on this as on everything. But I tried.

"I've told you once, I've told you a thousand times."

"Mrs Kennedy, you've told me nothing at all. I'm not trying to get any secrets out of you. Just that if I knew when she was last seen then I could go on from there."

"Could you now?"

"Yes. Check bus timetables and railway timetables and taxis . . ."

"What would she want with a taxi?"

". . . and pick up the thread. Don't you want to help me do that?"

"What do you think I feel? I'm a mother. Nobody knows my feelings in all this."

"I'm trying to help."

"You're stirring it up and upsetting everybody. I thought you were a gentleman."

"Don't you want to find her?"

"Who do you think you are? Talking to a mother like that! She's my blood and bone – don't forget that! You have a bloody great cheek whether you're a gentleman or not."

"You *must* remember when you saw her last. You *must*!"

"Of course I do. What do you take me for? Of course I do! It was a Tuesday!" Your mother was most emphatic. "Tuesday morning – off to work without a care in the world."

"You don't remember the date?"

"I've told you. A Tuesday."

But the girls in the office had seen you last on the Thursday.

Back home – having left your mother thanking me for the gift of a bottle of whisky and awash in copiously sincere tears – I tried to work it out. Either your mother had forgotten the day (I was pretty sure the girls in the office were accurate) or you had deliberately fudged the issue – stayed out for two nights – you could have claimed a girlfriend – and so laid a rather more complicated trail.

Whom could you have stayed with?

A new flare of suspicion went up like a distress signal. Perhaps there was another man, a man who had been around for months, the man of my suspicions. In which case – how easy to stay with him. He could have taken you away.

And he could be the father of the child! By now I 'knew' there was a child.

"You were her only boyfriend," said Mrs Kennedy the next day, repeatedly, her hand on my knee. "She thought the world of you. You were all she could ever wish for. She told me that." Both of us were attacking the scotch. "She said, 'This is it, Mam. This is it. He's the one.' A pity he's married, I said, but times are changing and I'm not old-fashioned and if he and you are of one mind – you'll get nothing but help from me. She's a good girl, Bernadette. Thank you. No water. Always a special favourite. And what if he is rich, a bank manager, I said. There's nothing wrong with that. You won't find the Kennedys turning against him for that . . . ."

So where were you, Bernadette? Now I know, but then – I wandered around, let me not exaggerate, so much worse has happened to so many people, but we have to speak for our own small lives – I wandered around like a lost soul. I had no centre to my life save for schemes to find you – none of which worked. You were elsewhere. With my, with our child. But where? Where? Then I saw you.

There. On the main street. Thinner, ill-looking, changed; but *you*.

EIGHTEEN

I suppose you must have worked out what to do when we met.
To me it was that rare occurrence – a complete surprise. You,
coming back to the town, must have anticipated it and prepared
for it. Which is to say you did not turn and run for your life as
this unwashed over-bearded (grey) smelly man approached you
with tears already gathered in mid-afternoon bloodshot eyes.
Only later did I see myself as I really was and only now can I
appreciate your poise when we met. You stood, a little shaky,
but you stood your ground. As I approached you I looked at
your belly. You could not miss the enquiry in that look and your
gaze followed mine and you blushed. My heart leapt up: I held
out both hands and awkwardly – it was the High Street – you
took them, briefly, like a glancing Papal touch.

It was you, I think, who suggested we drive down to the
Solway, to the sea. I would have suggested the Lakes but I can
see now that the pressure of old associations would have been
too confusing. The sea was an escape, it could wash us all away,
with salt enough to need no more tears.

You appeared not to notice the dereliction of my row of
terraced cottages. I was suddenly ashamed of them and simultaneously ashamed of what I saw I looked like. I did not invite
you in – how could I? – but mumbled a promise out of you to
wait for a few minutes. As I hacked at my beard first with
scissors and then with an oversharp razor and scalding water I
looked out to keep an eye on you – lashing myself for being so
stupid as to leave you alone after all that fearful absence but
simply unable to accompany you in that dosser condition. I
wanted to be the man you had known. I *had* to be him. I changed
clothes throughout, hurling water on myself, under my armpits,
splashing my groin, sluicing my chest, slopping it over my back,

towel pummelling, and arrived minutes later blood speckled about my neck, the tiny scarlet pricks already damaging the clean white collar.

You smiled, but rather wanly, and I tried to settle myself and understand your mood. It was not easy. I wanted to stop the car, throw my arms around you, bury my hands in your body and make love to you so blackly that everything between the last time and this time would be erased. Why did I not do it? You forbade it. There was a distance and I, in a labyrinth of perplexed emotions, had not the will or the energy to break it down and bring us coupled together. If I had done that would it have been better? Did you secretly want that? Did my politeness fail you?

We drove beyond the pines onto a path which led through the dunes. It was a mild spring, promising summer, following the afternoon showers, one of those piercingly clear evening views you can get across the Solway Firth. Scotland seemed near enough to touch. We were in the land of Roman milecastles and bloody Border wars – where the Kennedys came from – wastelands, debatable lands, and the sea ready to take away the dead as it had done so often before.

You asked for my handkerchief, licked one corner of it and dabbed at my neck and chin.

"I've been going mad," I said, while you were doing this, "looking for you."

You nodded, gave me back the handkerchief and walked a few paces ahead. The tide was out, the rippled sand glistening but firm underfoot.

"I was very sorry to hear about your wife," you said. "I just heard the other day. I'm very sorry."

"How did you hear?"

"I used to write to my mother now and then – just to tell her I was OK. And she would write back."

"So she knew where you were." There was no reply. "Why wouldn't she tell me?"

"I told her not to."

"I was almost out of my mind."

"That's what she said."

"Is that why you came back?"

Again, no reply. The gulls called out, the sea across the flat sands surged its distant rhythm. We were strolling, very slowly, side by side, stopping every now and then.

"Do you want to talk?"

"Not really," you said. Why did I not listen? "It's such a lovely evening. Nobody around but us. Much nicer just to walk without talking . . . But you can't do that, can you?"

"No. Is here a good place?"

"As good as any."

I detected even then a new tone in your voice. Wiser, I think; rather more resigned but wiser and, inevitably, sadder.

And of course having decided to talk, the talk that was imperative, the talk that would heal the wounds of the last months, I found that I had nothing to say and we walked along again in silence which could have been pleasant had I not had this compulsion that a talk had to be undergone.

"Where were you?"

"Here," you said, pointing south towards the pines where you had once raced away from me. "Staying with my 'sister' for the first weeks."

"Why did you leave the town?"

"Do you want me to tell you the truth – all the time?"

"Of course."

"It would be easier to miss things out."

"I'm OK now. I can manage," I said.

"I was talking about myself." You paused and then you resolved my confusion. "I saw how devoted you were to your wife. Christopher made a point of telling me and so, it appeared, did half the town. You practically lived in the hospital. Nothing was too much trouble. Nothing too good for her. I could admire it – I *did* admire it – and I understood that you had to behave like that – but I couldn't take it."

"It didn't affect what I felt for you."

"No . . ? You went to a flower shop right at the beginning, remember? – to get flowers for your wife, I presume. And you bought some for me as well – really very kind – sent them tactfully to home and not to work. But I thought: I'm on the side, I'm secondary, and that's fine, that's perfectly right. But I hated it. You had never made me feel like that before." You smiled. "Anyway I hate cut flowers. They're already dead, aren't they?"

"I know."

"Do you? Do you know how badly I behaved in my head? I dare not tell you about that. But I did keep thinking – surely there will be a little time left over for me – selfish, selfish – but just a *little*."

"How could I see you – when to see you might have meant never seeing Angela again? That was the point."

"I understand. I do. But I found it impossible to accept. So I left."

"Without telling me."

"That's right."

We walked on. The dusk was thickening but there was plenty of light on the sea. The isolation of the place seemed a comfort.

"Do you know we have been together all this time and we haven't even touched each other?"

"I never thought you'd ask!"

For some moments it was as it had been. And that was the last time. On that empty border shore.

"You said you were here for the first weeks. What happened then?"

"I'm cold. Could we go back to the car?"

"Yes."

I put my jacket around your shoulders but you were still cold when we got in the car. I offered to go to the big hotel nearby for a drink but "Better not," you said. I turned on the engine to warm up the car. Outside the night raced in as if it were a wind blowing in from the sea and the beach was desolate, the gulls' hawking mournful.

"I went over to Newcastle," you said.

"You couldn't face coming back?"

"No."

"Did you tell your mother where you were going?"

"Not at first. Not until I got settled. I had some money saved. You've never let me pay for a thing."

"What did you do there?"

"Got a job temping in the university. The Administration Department. It turned out to be useful. There was a noticeboard

full of offers of flats to share and I was soon settled in with two
others who weren't nosey. That was a relief."

You were finding it very difficult to talk and as you went on
my palate became dry. I can recall it precisely. I can take it. A
caked dryness; when I ran my tongue over it the sensation was
that of something frozen though not icy, not even cold. But stiff
in the same way.

"Why was it such a great relief?"

". . . I was pregnant."

In that second I realised that what I wanted even more than
you was us. That a child by, with, from you; a child to, for and
with us would be all the future I would ever want. And this child
– boy? girl? – this living creature made by our making love . . . I
felt drowsy with the deepest movement of pleasure and yet
your tone kept me fearful.

"Why didn't you tell me?" A whisper – or not much above a
whisper – was all I could manage.

"I couldn't. You were bound up with your wife. It wouldn't
have been fair on you, or her. I'd promised to keep away."

"But not if you were pregnant. That changed everything,
didn't it? That's a new life. New rules. Just to tell me – so that
I could have helped – or just known . . ."

"How long would it go on, though? Your wife's illness – how
long would it go on? How long would I have to wait?"

"I don't know. But what did it matter? There would be our
child."

"What sort of life would the child have had? What life could it
have had? How could I shame you in front of everybody – and
your wife so ill, everybody saying what a saint she was, what a
saint you were, what sort of life could it ever have had? I did it
for you, don't you understand that?"

"Bernadette . . ."

"*No* life! No life without you. I had so many black days.
Thinking I would never, ever see you again. Where were you?
Why did you not just . . . let me know that I mattered to you?
For how long could I have waited with a child?"

"Bernadette!"

"It would have had no life. No father. No life. No chance. I
was in no state."

"Bernadette. No! It was my child too."

"I didn't mean to."

"Why the – why on earth *did* – oh God!"

"This Canadian medical student – working – like me – there – noticed how upset – he was very nice – one day – and said it was painless these days, it was not too far gone, nobody need know."

"Why did you not tell me?"

"I had to do it. You were not there. Perhaps you never would be there."

"It was my child as well! It was our child but it was my child as well! I could have been a good father. We could have had a fine child, a good – it doesn't matter – just *our* child. Why did you not tell me? How could you do all that – how could you take a life, part of my life – how could you do that without telling me? What had I ever – what had I *ever* done to you that made you think I would let you down? You must think me such a – what *do* you think? I would have found a way to make it work."

"If only I'd known."

"That Angela would die so soon?" That was cruel.

"Yes."

"So. It was all a matter of timing and calculation, was it? How long did you give her? Six months – OK, have the child. Nine months – a little dicey! Twelve months – a positive worry. More than that – well, if she's going to hang on all that time and they keep discovering these new cures for cancer – let's get rid of it, out! Out! Out it goes."

You were crying by then. I may have been crying too. But I could not relent.

"How could you *do* it? Do you have *all* the rights all the time? Why don't you get artificially inseminated next time round and do it properly? Who needs a poor sod of a man when there are sperm banks all over the western world? I see. I have no rights. None at all. *And neither does the child!* I thought you were a Catholic. I won't make such claims but I am not a cipher. I was the father of that once-to-be-a-child – yes?"

"Oh yes. How could you ask? How *could* you? Don't you see I thought I did it for you, for us? The father? Don't you *see*?

Yes, the father. Yes. Yes!" Your sobbing ought to have moved me: but I was out of control.

"Yes nothing. I was nothing. Like that child's life. You murdered it."

And then – oh dearest Bernadette – I turned to you in that car, caught you by the throat and shook and shook you until you burst loose and screamed more stridently than the gulls.

I drove back very carefully and left you outside your mother's house. We exchanged not one more word.

A final humiliation.

I walked down to your house the next night determined to apologise. I bought some flowers but some way along the road remembered what you had said about cut flowers and threw them in the river. I had thought everything through as hard as I could and I could see your side. You were alone. Your family would have raised hell if you had admitted being pregnant; and after that they would have come for me. You truly thought that such a course would further distress Angela and be an unfair burden on me. You had thought it through. Besides, as you had so honestly confessed – you felt lonely and unjustly abandoned. I understood that also. Balance of mind disturbed.

The only sane thing to do was to go forward I thought as I pressed on towards your house, wishing I had brought the car and not been diverted by the sobering thought of a walk. More urgently, I began to fear that you might have left the town again, indeed you might be leaving at this very minute. I broke into a run and almost as soon broke into a sweat: I had been drinking hard.

Your mother gave me three inches of hallway view as she opened the door and said you would not see me.

"But she has to."

"She makes her own mind up."

"I've things to say to her."

"The state of her last night you'd said quite enough and me thinking you were a regular bank manager."

"Let me at least speak to her here. At the door."

"She wants nothing more to do with you."

"I don't believe that. I just don't believe that."

"Are you doubting my word?"

Mrs Kennedy was known to be aggressive come the occasion and now she showed her form.

"Yes," I said, as I thought evenly but I may, as they claimed later, have begun to shout and swear. "Why the hell should I *not* doubt your word when you lied to me day in and day bloody out about Bernadette?"

"I was looking after her best interests."

"Like hell you were. You were looking after your own interests like you always have done. You'd have sold her down the river for a few quid if you could have done. You tried it once – didn't you? Don't deny it. You bloody did, didn't you? And nearly ruined her life in the process! Well?"

The door banged in my face but I hammered on it still yelling, still calling for you until Theresa came to the door – just as angry as her mother (the men were out, thank God) and began to lash out at my face, trying to scratch my eyes out, I presume. I don't blame her. But when her mother came and pretended I was attacking Theresa and joined in the assault I retreated down the cracked cement which was the garden path.

By then neighbours, no doubt well used to the job, had called the police – no doubt used to coming to the Kennedys but not quite for this circumstance. They took me home. The younger constable advised me to "Get those scratches seen to."

It was Joe who sought me out and said that if I bothered you again, Theresa and your mother would prefer charges, that *you* would dearly like me to leave the town but failing that, or until that could be arranged, I was to keep out of your way and never approach you, never speak to you. And the pub was out of bounds or he himself would be forced to take steps, very sorry and all that, pal, but there we were.

So I took a little of my life in my hands when I saw you today, Bernadette. I thought I tracked you quite skilfully. You did not seem to notice me which was the best I could hope for. You are a little more of your old self. Spring suits you. Your body is tense but now and then the hip juts a little forward, the breasts swing slightly, the hair lifts to the lift of your walk. So that could be the last time.

The plain truth is that I 'love you to death'. It was an expression older people used in my childhood but I can apply it to myself now. Without you – oh, I won't do anything silly, but life will be nothing but a series of mechanical manoeuvres: getting by. Waiting for it to be over and making sure never to upset you again. You see, I did not only put all I had into you, I put more than I imagined I could ever have and I received in turn more than I could have dared to dream of. We were wonderfully, totally, fast in love, Bernadette, and nothing, nothing on earth can ever replace it.

NINETEEN

My dearest Bernadette,

I have written you a very long letter. It talks about us and our life. You will not read it – that is if you want to – until you pick it up from the safety box in which I will deposit it in Carlisle. The bank taught me a good copperplate hand and I think you will find it legible. I wanted there to be a record, my record, of what happened. I wanted you to know about what I felt for you but in the end it is indescribable. You were the light, you were also the darkest richness of sex, you were the fun of the day and the ambiguities of twilight: I was, I am, I will forever be, in love with you.

But I woke up the other morning and saw more clearly. Like a ship hitting calmer waters I suppose. Same ship, same baggage, same sea: but calmer. I could no longer persecute you by hanging about the town, a drunken clown, embarrassing you by my presence. For however strictly I kept to my promise to Big Joe you must always have feared that I would appear around a corner, ambush you in a shop, hold you up on that last lonely stretch to your house; from being a friendly place, the town must have become a minefield. I had to leave you alone. That much was clear and that was all I needed. And I cut down on the whisky.

I did all this because I could not control the force of what I feel for you – that is my excuse for what I am about to do. How quickly a powerful and good feeling can cause violent pain if it does not find a proper course! Ours seemed to have a chance. Oh, Bernadette – let me cut through this. I love you to death and yet I must go and leave you alone. There will be no one else. You occupy all my heart. The memory of you will be a stronger force in me for the rest of my life than the actual physical presence of any other human being. And what I have I value. I would not change it for anything on earth but the reality of you.

We met on a practical note. Let us end on one.

I have deposited money for you in that bank in Carlisle – the Lowther Street branch of my own bank – which holds the long document or letter I have written you and one or two other mementoes. The money involved is a large sum – not only by your standards but by the standards of anyone in the town. Very large – it may alarm you – but I can afford it. I still have quite enough and more left over for my most ambitious needs. You will find a second letter which outlines what I think is the best way to invest this so that it can be of considerable long-term advantage to you. If you choose to ignore it *please* do so. Blow the lot! It is yours now. But if you would like further advice, ask for Mr Coates, the assistant manager. He is thoroughly reliable and discreet: he spent three years working for me! When you first go down, don't be shy; just ask any cashier if you can see Mr Coates: Miss Kennedy is here to see him. Late mornings (pre-12.30) is his best time. Any time in the next three months.

I am delivering this letter to you by hand but in the early hours so you will not know that I have been and gone. It would be unfair just to disappear and so I will be here until tomorrow night at 8.00 p.m. in case you want to reply. After that I drive to Edinburgh where the hotel expects me about 10.30 which means I can have a nightcap and go straight to bed. After that, I intend to go up the West Coast of Scotland – *terra incognita* as far as I'm concerned but I've heard it holds fine landscapes and long beaches: I would like to find empty sandy beaches for strolling.

So there we are, my darling. Where did you come from? What would life have been without you? A poor thing. Thank you for that.

I'll end now. Goodbye. Good luck. I love you and there cannot be anyone else.

I was more in control now. I found that organising my departure was quite soothing. I had cut down on the whisky without strain

– less than half a bottle a day. I did not want to fall too much below that – it was a certain pleasure and they are few.

I was so exhausted on one level, and so afraid that my strength might fail me before I did what I knew I had to do that organisational matters were a blessing. But after I had written and delivered that letter to you I was at a loss. I had organised someone to keep Angela's grave tidy: the same man who looked after her mother's and my mother's. The good furniture was well stored. The rest would go in the next sale and the proceeds be put in my account. I had paid up my rent on the condemned terraced cottage for which I now discovered I had a certain affection: it had been a refuge. I was on my way.

But where? And why? And why alone? Questions like these had to be banished. But I was only intermittently good at that act of despotism.

Of course I had 'given' you the two days in order to give myself a last chance. How many gifts of love are unselfish? Perhaps pure selfishness is integral to true love. But I had given myself the problem of those two days. How to blot them up?

I went back into the Lake District. I did something I had never done before – I motored all over the map of it. Round any lake which could be rounded, through any pass which could be surmounted, gliding off onto byways, seeking out remote places: two days of enforced concentration on the business of driving on narrow twisting roads alleviated by prospects which have never let me down. I avoided staying the night at any hotel which had witnessed our nights, but found a perfectly acceptable bed and breakfast near Grasmere.

Back in the town at seven, I filled up with petrol and went home. I would observe the eight o'clock deadline. I looked at my pre-packed luggage, and then sat down on the chair I would bequeath to the cottage's future tenant. Only then did I notice the envelope which had been slid under the door and lodged itself under the rush matting. Just a corner was showing. You began with no frills:

It is a time for the truth but how difficult it is to pin it down. What we said to each other and did to each other at our best seems so far away now. Was that really us?

Let me come to the heart of it. After what happened
to me as a girl I felt unclean and untouchable. Thanks
to a lot of help from that teacher in particular I finally
got through the tough part. I put on a hard face
and followed the Kennedy track – which can
be a help in its peculiar way – and I was coming
through.

Then there was you and, as I wrote, I fell in love with
you. Now I see that it was partly because you, I
thought, could bring back or bring into life something
like the innocence that had been torn away. You made me
feel valuable and gave me the good things. These had
been taken away from me – my life would never have
them because of one stupid man and, yes, one stupid
mother. But she is still my mother.

All I ever dreamed of was to be fine – will you laugh
if I say 'a good girl'? I mean – this is 1990 and what
we younger generation don't know about drugs, Aids,
sex, obscenities, violence – what we don't know about
all that is 'like, you know', not worth knowing. So they
say.

I don't want all that. I want to feel decent, I want
to have a life I can look up to and not flinch away
from.

In Newcastle I went to a church and tried to pray. I
wanted God to tell me whether or not to keep the baby.
I never found it easy to pray – I don't know why. At
first, for a few minutes, there was such a relief that I felt
that God was indeed listening to my prayers. I even
felt – in that moment – that I could go to confession and
perhaps take communion. But it passed. I went twice
more to the church but that feeling never returned and
what persisted was that I could not look to the faith
unless I was truly sorry about us. I could not feel that.
So I was barred. But then I had been an outcast from
decency until you appeared and convinced me that you
were in love with me. I thought I had ruined it by being
so crass and nervous and giving in right away but you
went on and on being understanding and finally I knew

that it was good. With you I could have a real life. I
would be honest and open about it: it would feel worth
something.

And then your wife. And my pregnancy. And her
death. And the abortion. It all collapsed.

I read Jane Austen at school and when I was over in
Newcastle under the worst pressure, I bought the
paperbacks and read her again. I wanted to be like one
of her heroines! How stupid that must sound – from my
background, with my family, our awful record, a million
miles from Jane Austen and yet I longed to be someone
as *true* as her heroines. You made me feel something
like that – even though the sex would not have pleased
her at all! Maybe we got that wrong too. Maybe we
should have waited.

I've already told you what a blackout for me those
very first times were. I thought it would always be
like that. When the girls (not in the office – Theresa and
her friends) talk about it, they either yell with laughter
or complain. I thought it was what you had to put up
with to earn the good bits. But when you just lay beside
me that first night in the boarding-house I remember
being hungry for you and terrified that you were so
angry about the guitar business in the pub that you were
just counting the hours to get away from me. I
remember feeling hot and aching in a way which I could
not recognise: I wanted you. I wanted you. But you just
lay there, flat on your back, like a Pharaoh on his tomb.
I was convinced you had gone off me for good.

When I cried the next morning it wasn't put on. I
thought I had ruined everything. What followed was
utterly amazing. I've never told you enough how much
I love the way we made love. I love it. I *love* it. It was like
nothing I'd heard from the girls, a *bit* like some of the
things I've read if I'm honest, but mostly it was new and
it *was* amazing. I love to touch you as much as you
wanted to touch me. And doing it – just keeping on
doing it. You were always so intense and I realised that
was because you meant it so much; nobody can lie

about that. So that was the truth and I loved knowing it
was the truth. Sometimes we were doing so much to
each other I thought I would explode. It was like a
current of water rippling just under my skin, a
swayboat taking my feelings up in the air and swooping
them down again and always the *pleasure*. I was greedy.
After you'd fallen asleep I would wait for the first sign
to wake you up again. On those informative walks of
yours I was scouting ahead for likely spots! Back home
on my own I would go to bed early just so I could go over
it again and again. I still do. I was mad about what we
did together. It was like finding a spring that just
flowed and flowed on. But now what I think about *most*
is not the sex – though I miss it and memories can still
make me flush; but what I miss is just your stroking me.
You used to do it when you thought I was asleep and
I would pretend to be asleep so that you wouldn't stop.
We would be in bed, past the middle of the night, like
a pair of spoons – and you would touch my hair, very
very gently touch it, stream your fingers through it as if
you were patiently untangling it. Then the pads of your
fingertips would steal down my back, scarcely brushing
the skin in case you disturbed me. I can feel it now,
blind hands, dark skin, both of us silent, my willing
myself not to break the spell. Your hand would go down
and round cupping my bottom to my thighs, as if you were
just discovering me or making sure. It was the most
loving thing you ever did and today I wake up miserable
that I have lost it. You always ended the same way:
kissed my hair lightly – perhaps you thought a kiss on
the skin would impose too much – and then you rested
a hand on the valley between my hips and ribs. I loved
that; I love it now. And it was what it led to. I was free,
all of a sudden. Instead of being closed in on myself,
I was open to all sorts of things. Like coming out of a
coal-cellar into sunshine. And – don't laugh –
everything seemed to have music in it. Those walks
we took, the sunsets we looked at, I was not bolted
in on myself any more. You had pulled me into a different

world and sex was somehow the key to it. But just with you. Still with you.

Could we go back to the beginning? Could we court each other, could we not forget but forgive the past, could we . . . ? And you have given me a dowry – so you write. I want to spend it on us. Can I take you to Paris? I always wanted to go: that was what the Rotary Prize was supposed to buy. Remember?!

I just want to be with you for ever and feel decent, feel that I was worth something.

I will be honest. The operation was not as easy as my Canadian friend had promised. I still wake up crying about it.

I know now that I was wrong not to keep the child. I don't want an explanation to sound like an excuse but I owe you more than I could give you that time.

I was ashamed of myself, being pregnant, and thought you would be ashamed of me too. I couldn't bear the idea of that. It was wrong to let what you thought of me push everything else out of the way but there was nothing I could do about it. I'm sorry. What would you *think* of me? Common as dirt, just what I always feared you might think. Even when we were in bed and it was so *good* I still thought sometimes, "He thinks I'm *bad*." I even worried, at first, that you liked me *because* I was bad. So to turn up on your doorstep pregnant would ruin it all. "Typical," they could say, "of a Kennedy!"

I don't want you to be sorry for me but I *was* scared. I left home and then went away altogether so that you would suffer no scandal. You were being so good to your wife – this would've just spoiled it. And then I panicked.

When would you be free? Would you then still love me? My mother was not encouraging – she said that as you never wrote (which I understood) that proved I had been no more than a fling. If you *had* gone off me and I did have your child would that not seem a way of blackmailing you? Because you would certainly have come forward with money to help whether you loved me or not and I could not bear to be seen to be milking you. I

did not know how to behave. My family would have
'killed me' but they would have coped in the end. But I
became convinced I would have lost you. Not to lose
you became an obsession.

Do you have any idea of the way an obsession controls
your mind? I would guess you do. So you know that it is
as if someone has plugged in to you. All that I heard
were your words, all that I saw was your face – and
your body, I missed that, I missed your touching me
and exciting me so much, wanting to take me entirely,
wanting to have me, to do me until you were exhausted
and I was too but we both wanted more – I could not
block you out. You mattered more than anyone; more
than my life. But you were with someone else – perhaps
for years. How could I hold on to you or at least not
lose you? I would have done anything not to lose you. I
did the worst thing I could have done and I have hurt
you too much to mend. I had the abortion for love of
you and it has killed that love for ever.

Your letter moves me so much. Why do you want me
to have money? Writing a letter on my investments!
Typical. Lovely. Loving. Telling me your itinerary. Was
that the last temptation? Edinburgh; the Western
Isles? You are so sweet and transparent sometimes that
I feel that I am in my fifties and you just past nineteen
(you missed the birthday: still, I *was* in Newcastle!).

But I have hurt you too much. I can never forget what
you said and did when I told you how I had dealt with the
pregnancy. I think you were right, you see. Now I
understand it. Do I, will I always, understand what
matters most too late? I can't live in the shadow of your
unforgivingness. Nor can I expect you to make me
feel clean any more. That must be my own business.

There has to be a place for people like me. People
who want love and are capable of it. People who don't
give a damn about fashions and smartness but want
devotion, caring and being cared for, a life open to
simple things like the walks we took. And people who
are badly flawed – as I am – we want that too. We want

a chance to mend and reach out for the best – not the richest – the best. You gave me that chance. You took me to that place. I will always love you for it. Always.

    I can write no more. Good luck my love. Take care,
                        Bernadette.

I felt the heat come from your letter like a blush. I understood. There was nothing to forgive. You will soon realise that. We had a life together if only we could take it, if only our fingers could touch and interlock and hold on across this chasm of time and injury which had forced us apart. I began by writing that I wanted to cast a spell on you. Your final letter seemed the answer to my efforts. You were as eager as I was. You will be there when I go out.

    I will seal this and send it off to the safe deposit. I will lock the door and put the keys through the letter box as arranged. Then, in the evening spring darkness I will take my suitcases over to the car. I *know* that you will be there. Your hair swaying down past your shoulders. Those eyes – that healing mouth. Will you? Darling. Bernadette.

MELVYN BRAGG

THE MAID OF BUTTERMERE

'A triumph . . . I am overwhelmingly impressed'
Beryl Bainbridge

'An ingenious telling of a romantic tragedy'
Gore Vidal

'A detailed, eloquent and affecting panorama of truth and lies
. . . His new novel thrusts him into the front rank'
David Hughes in The Mail on Sunday

'This is the story of an impostor and bigamist, a self-styled
Colonel Hope, who travels to the North, where eventually he
marries "The Maid of Buttermere", a young woman whose
natural beauty inspired the dreams and confirmed the theories
of various early nineteenth century writers . . . It is a fine
story . . . This is historical fiction with a human face'
Peter Ackroyd in The Times

'Very much enjoyed; a fine subject treated with great energy
and imagination, and a gusto that Hazlitt would have admired'
Richard Holmes

'A vivid and erudite historical *tour de force* – romantic fiction for
the thinking reader'
Penelope Lively

'Bragg achieves the most difficult feats, the telling of the
changing perceptions and ideals of a radical age . . . He is also
as powerful as ever in his description of nature'
Andrew Sinclair in The Sunday Times

'A skilled, ornate and convincing examination of a nineteenth-
century scandal in Bragg's own Cumbria'
Thomas Keneally

sceptre